THE WIND
CHILDREN

THE WIND CHILDREN

CHILDREN

AND OTHER TALES FROM JAPAN

retold by
Samira Kirollos

Illustrated by
YUKKI YAURA

ANDRE DEUTSCH

First published in 1989 by
André Deutsch Limited
105-106 Great Russell Street, London WC1B 3LJ

ISBN Hardback 0 233 98408 9
ISBN paperback 0 233 98442 9

Printed in Great Britain by
Ebenezer Baylis and Son Limited, Worcester

To Tim
for his understanding

CONTENTS

ACKNOWLEDGEMENTS

The author would like to thank the following:

Celia Clear, Managing Editor of British Museum Publications and John Reeve, Head of Education at the British Museum for their encouragement and support.

Maurice Coyaud for his advice and for permitting me to use some of his translations.

Margaret Leona for her perceptive comments on the first draft of the book. Norman Longmate for helping me with the bibliography. My editor, Pamela Royds, for her useful suggestions. Simon Hayward of the Japan National Tourist Organization for advice and assistance. Japan Air Lines whose generous help allowed me to undertake the research trip to Japan.

My Japanese students who, through their trust have offered me, over the years, an invaluable insight into Japan and the Japanese. All those in Japan who guided me so painstakingly and with such kindness and generosity through Izumo, Matsue, Osaka, Kyōto, Matsuyama, Kanazawa, Sapporo, Sendai and last, but certainly not least, Tōkyō.

Shippeitarō

Hundreds of years ago, in old Japan, there lived a brave, good looking, young samurai warrior named Chōshirō. His father and mother were in good health. There were no wars to fight. He was not married.

As Chōshirō's life was calm and uneventful and he had no immediate responsibilities, he decided to leave the large estate on which he lived with his parents to go off in search of adventure. Since leaving home was character building, his parents did not mind his going away for some time.

As Chōshirō walked through the dark, green forest, he wondered if he would meet a fox-woman. He had often heard that foxes disguised themselves as women to put you into all sorts of trouble. He felt a thrill in the pit of his stomach at the thought of their tricks.

As he walked alongside rivers and ponds, he wondered if he would meet a yellow-green, monkey-like, water imp, commonly known as a Kappa. At the thought of a Kappa, Chōshirō flexed his muscles. Kappas were known to enjoy wrestling with human beings. That would really be a challenge.

As Chōshirō walked onto an open plain, he looked out for the huge, red, blue, pink or grey Oni, a devil-like creature, with horns, three toes, three fingers and three eyes. Chōshirō imagined the dangers he would face should he meet an Oni.

As the courageous samurai climbed up a mountain he looked at the sky to see whether he would see the winged, beaked Tengu with its red cloak and small black hat come flying over his head.

What tricks would the Tengu play on him?

Every time night fell, Chōshirō would begin to wonder if he might be visited by the legless, shadowless, long-haired, pale-faced, white-robed ghosts of samurai warriors or their wives who had died long ago. These ghosts could make your hair stand on end.

But during the time that Chōshirō walked on and on for seven days in search of adventure, he saw no foxes, no Kappas, no Onis, no Tengus, no ghosts.

On the evening of the seventh day, Chōshirō walked through a dark forest and up a lonely mountain. There he saw no solitary huts and no lonely villages. The path he was walking on ended abruptly and he found himself having to fight his way through thorny brambles. After some time, he saw a clearing and there, in front of him, stood a spooky little temple. There was nothing and no one in it. It was entirely in ruins.

It started to rain heavily, so Chōshirō decided to call it a day and stop looking for a hut or a village where he could find food. He lay down on his back, on the floor, behind the temple door, his two good swords placed safely alongside his body.

"Well, this is my seventh night away from home," Chōshirō thought. "I set off in search of adventure and have so far found nothing. I'd better give myself a good night's sleep. Who knows what tomorrow will bring!"

3

Chōshirō sent himself to sleep by dreaming up adventures in his mind's eye. At midnight precisely, he was woken up by the most awful sounds. They were spine-chilling, blood curdling noises. The loud, piercing yells and shrieks and miaowing of cats went right through his ears into his brain. His head throbbed. He thought he would go deaf.

Clutching his sword, Chōshirō edged his way along the wall till he found an enormous hole in the hollow of a huge pine tree which stood next to the temple. He quickly hid in it and watched.

"Well I never," thought Chōshirō, "nine old white cats. These old cats are known to be magical, and can be terribly dangerous. People fear them, because, for one thing, they can understand the speech of human beings! What on earth are they doing . . . dancing on their tails like that! Good Lord! They are surely the cats that have the power to kill human beings."

The nine cats looked really weird. Three were wearing hats, three held fans and three wore head-bands.

No sooner had Chōshirō thought these thoughts than he heard the nine white cats miaow in unison:

> "Shippeitarō. Shippeitarō.
> Where are you?
> Where are you?
> Where?
> Where?
> Where?"

One of the three cats who were wearing hats said:

> "Shippeitarō will not come tonight.
> He will not.
> He will not."

The doors of the temple opened mysteriously all by themselves.

The three cats who were holding fans walked into the temple, ahead of the others, quietly, in single file.

They were followed by the three cats who were wearing hats.

These in turn were followed by the three cats who were wearing head bands.

4

Luckily, Chōshirō was well hidden in the hollow of the pine tree. He was in an excellent position to see everything that was going on without being seen.

Once they got into the temple, the nine white cats held hands and formed a circle. They chanted this strange, rhythmic song which echoed eerily throughout the temple.

> "Do not tell. Do not tell.
> To Shippeitarō.
> To Shippeitarō.
> Do not tell. Do not tell.
> To Schippeitarō.
> If we tell. If we tell.
>
> It will be our hell.
> It will be our hell.
>
> So . . .
>
> Do not tell. Do not tell.
> To Shippeitarō.
> To Schippeitarō."

On and on and on the cats sang and danced. They repeated this weird song with rhythmic monotony as they danced on their tails.

After some time, they walked out of the temple in threes, the same way as they had come in. The nine, white ghost cats tiptoed away and disappeared into the night.

It was now some time past midnight.

"I wonder who Shippeitarō is," thought Chōshirō. "He must possess supernatural powers. Those wretched white ghost cats are afraid of him. He can surely kill them. I wonder, I just wonder what mischief or evil these cats have been up to."

With these thoughts Chōshirō, the brave samurai warrior, fearlessly went back to sleep in the same place, behind the temple door, his two good swords placed safely alongside his body.

It was late morning when Chōshirō woke up with the sun shining on his face. He felt completely refreshed.

"I had better find a village soon as I am ravenously hungry. Also, I'd better not spend another night here. I don't much like the idea of these nine cats. Besides, what kind of adventure is there for me in their boring singing and dancing?"

As Chōshirō began to walk away from the temple, he saw a path clearly traced ahead of him which had, most certainly, not been there the day before. Chōshirō did not question too much its strange, sudden appearance but simply thought: "I'm glad it's leading onto an open plain and not into the forest. I feel like being in open spaces."

On his way, Chōshirō passed by some isolated huts where the farmers were cooking o-mochi (chewy rice cakes). The humble, generous people willingly shared some of their o-mochi with him.

Chōshirō kept pressing on until he came to a large mansion situated on the outskirts of a small village. There was no smell of o-mochi rising from the large house as had been the case with the other houses. There was total silence in and around the mansion. It was like a ghost house. Chōshirō had the impression that no one was living in it at all, but as he drew closer to it he could hear the sound of many people crying softly.

"That is really strange," thought Chōshirō. "What is going on?" He entered the house and found a family sitting on their knees. The father, mother, three boys and the servants were crying as they sat around a young girl.

"Why are you crying?" Chōshirō asked them with great concern.

"Oh, it is too awful, too awful to tell," the mother said in a flood of tears.

"Perhaps I can help you," the young samurai suggested confidently. He had been brought up since early childhood on the old code of chivalry of his forefathers. The father looked at Chōshirō and although he knew that, being a samurai, Chōshirō did have great power and strength, still he said sadly, shaking his head: "No one can help us I'm afraid."

The mother explained: "Up there, up on that mountain in a ruined and deserted temple lives a mountain spirit. Every year, at harvest time, he demands that a young girl be offered to him. If we refuse to please him, a huge storm is created which destroys our rice fields and paddies. When that happens we begin to starve."

"This year," the girl's brother said, "it is my sister's turn to die. It's terrible. I do wish I could be killed instead of her."

When the young boy said these words the family started crying all over again.

Chōshirō prodded the family further: "Tell me more. How do you sacrifice your girl?"

"We always put the victim in a wooden box," the father explained. "Our strongest and bravest men take the girl to the ruined, deserted temple up on the mountain and leave her there overnight. In the morning when the men return to the box they always find that the girl has vanished . . . but completely. There is not one single little trace of her left."

"Does the temple have a huge pine tree with a hole within it so big a man can stand in it?"

"Yes it most certainly has," the father replied.

"I spent last night there, at the temple," Chōshirō stated calmly.

"You what?" the youngest brother asked with disbelief.

Chōshirō nodded his head and smiled then said: "May I ask you a question please? Who is Shippeitarō?"

"Shippeitarō? I'm sorry I cannot answer that question," the father said.

"How soon must your daughter be sacrificed?" Chōshirō asked further.

"In seven days' time," the mother answered.

"Could you please make me a small map of this region which indicates the villages and houses that surround your estate?"

Chōshirō was soon given the map. He decided to work his way around the villages in a circular journey going clockwise.

"Take good care of your daughter. Do not lose heart," Chōshirō told them comfortingly. "Goodbye."

Chōshirō went from village to village, house to house, asking everyone if they knew of a man called Shippeitarō. Unfortunately, no one seemed to know anyone of that name.

On the seventh day Chōshirō found that he had nearly completed his circle. He was worried and anxious about not being able to save the family from their coming tragedy. He was sitting with his thoughts on a stone, by a brook, when he heard a man's voice shout out authoritatively: "Shippeitarō! Shippeitarō! Come here!"

There, bouncing towards Chōshirō came a huge, strong looking, black and white dog. He was almost as big as a calf.

Chōshirō jumped up to his feet and with the extreme politeness of the samurai asked the man if he could borrow his dog.

It so happened that the elderly man who owned Shippeitarō was none other than the Daimyō . . . the lord of the area. He was, of course, reluctant to let a stranger borrow his favourite dog. Why should he? But Chōshirō was terribly insistent and begged and begged the Daimyō to let him borrow Shippeitarō . . . just for one night.

"Just for one night, then," the Daimyō consented at last. "You look like a trustworthy lad to me."

Of course the Daimyō knew that he was dealing with a samurai.

Chōshirō rushed back to the family with Shippeitarō. The family had given up on Chōshirō who had been away for seven days. They had dressed their daughter in a white kimono which meant death. They had placed her in a wooden box. The strong men of the village had already carried her half way up the mountain. Chōshirō was rapidly told what was happening and he and Shippeitarō soon caught up with the sad procession.

"Take the girl back home immediately," Chōshirō told the men. He was quite out of breath.

"Impossible," they answered fearfully. "The mountain spirit will destroy us and our land if we do such a thing. We cannot possibly take the girl back."

"Just do as I say," Chōshirō insisted. "Take her home and hide her. I am prepared to die instead of her. It is part of the samurai code of honour. All I need is for two or three of you to take that box up to the temple with me. That is all."

The men did as they were told. Half of them took the girl back to her family. The other half went up to the deserted temple.

Once they had placed the wooden chest inside the temple the men ran away down the mountain as fast as their legs could carry them, as though ghosts were chasing them away from such a spooky place.

Chōshirō placed Shippeitarō in the wooden chest. The highly intelligent dog, who was imbued with extraordinary powers, cooperated willingly. He seemed to understand and know instinctively what would be demanded of him. Chōshirō patted

Shippeitarō on the head then took up his hiding place in the hollow of the pine tree.

At midnight precisely, as the full moon shed its light on the entire mountainside and fog wrapped itself around the lower regions of the mountains, the nine, hideous, white ghost cats reappeared. This time they were being led by the most enormous black cat. He was three times their size and looked even fiercer and more terrible than the rest. His yellow eyes shone wickedly as he narrowed them to peer at the box.

Once again, the cats let out those awful bloodcurdling yells and shrieks as they circled round and round and round the box dancing on their tails. Once again they chanted ominously:

> "Do not tell. Do not tell.
> To Shippeitarō. To Shippeitarō.
> Do not tell. Do not tell.
> To Shippeitarō.
>
> If we tell. If we tell.
>
> It will be our hell.
> It will be our hell.
>
> So . . .
>
> Do not tell. Do not tell.
> To Shippeitarō.
> To Shippeitarō."

The cats then went into a frenzied dance around the box. They leapt high up into the air, made circles and landed on their tails. They yelled and made repulsive cries as they mocked at their victim while they built up their singing and dancing to a horrible climax. Suddenly . . . without any warning, the black cat lifted the lid of the wooden box.

Shippeitarō let out the most awful howl. The huge, strong dog pounced on the cat, flung him to the ground, and bit him hard on the throat.

In a flash, Chōshiro had leapt out of the pine tree and with a sure blow of his powerful, long sword, mercilessly cut off the

black cat's head. With his second sword Chōshirō slit the body of the cat in two, putting all his samurai power into the sword so that the cat would never come back . . . as cat or ghost.

The nine white cats were so stunned by the sudden appearance of Shippeitarō, the enemy they feared the most, as well as by the death of their master, the black cat, that they forgot to run away. They simply stood on the toes of their four legs, petrified, as though they had turned to marble.

Shippeitarō and Chōshirō finished them all off in no time.

Nine white bodies and a black one lay in a circle in front of the temple.

Chōshirō's samurai values and inner strength combined with Shippeitarō's good training and extraordinary powers meant that in the battle between good and evil, good had won and evil, in the form of the ten cats, would never come back to make the people suffer.

Chōshirō and Shippeitarō immediately went back to the family in the mansion, even though it was well past midnight, to give them the good news that the evil mountain spirit had been conquered once and for all. The ten dead cats, lying in a circle, their feet up in the air, their tails horizontal, their eyes glazed and expressionless, were sure proof of the truth of Chōshirō's story.

The fearless samurai warrior waited till morning to return the heroic Shippeitarō to his good master, the Daimyō. Chōshirō simply could not thank the Daimyō enough for having had the generosity to lend him his favourite dog. The Daimyō, on his part, thanked Chōshirō for having saved his area from the mountain fiend.

In time, Shippeitarō became as famous as any dog can be. As for the brave Chōshirō . . . well . . . he did not marry the girl whose life he saved as so often happens in folk tales.

He had had a splendid adventure, that is true, but he had only been away from home for two weeks and was not quite ready to go back yet. He saw a path at his feet leading onto an open plain. Without hesitation he took it in search of new and even more thrilling adventures.

Would he meet a fox woman, a Kappa, an Oni, a Tengu, a ghost or . . . another lot of cats?

The Wind Children

One crisp autumn day in a very poor village in Japan two boys and a girl played quietly in the courtyard of a temple. They were not brothers and sisters, but were good friends who came from three different families.

Their parents had gone to the fields to work hard so that they could provide their children with their daily bowl of rice. Every single day rice was the only thing they were given to eat. There never seemed to be any money for fish, vegetables, fruit or sweets.

A stranger flew down to the village on the wings of the wind. He walked over to the forecourt of the temple where the children were playing and told them: "You seem to have nothing to eat in this village. Why don't you come with me to a place where you will find thousands of delicious pears, persimmons and chestnuts? I can take you there easily. Would you like to go there?"

The stranger made this offer hundreds of years ago at a time, not like today, when it was safe to speak to and even go off with strangers. The eldest boy said: "Do you honestly know of such a place? If it really does exist, I'd love to come."

"I'd love to come, too," the youngest boy said eagerly.

"Me too," the girl cried out, jumping up and down. "Don't you dare leave me behind!"

The girl was younger than the eldest boy and older than the youngest boy.

"Come with me then," the stranger said smiling. "Come. Just hold me here."

He turned his back to the eldest boy. He took the child's hands and placed them at the side of his waist. The girl held the eldest boy in the same way. She was in turn held by the youngest boy.

The stranger blew into the air and in no time the three children flew off with him far, far up into the blue, cloudless sky.

They all landed in a dream place where they found thousands of pears, persimmons and chestnuts hanging on trees.

The stranger blew gently at the trees. As he did so, the fruit that was ripe fell down to the ground in glorious, delicious piles.

"Eat as much as you want," the stranger told them kindly.

The three children did not need to be asked twice. They ate and ate and ate to their heart's content . . . just short of getting stomach aches.

When they had had more than enough to eat, the girl asked the stranger: "Would you like us to teach you some of our games?"

For some time the stranger played happily with the well-fed children. Then as night fell, although he had not paid any attention whatsoever to time, he suddenly got up impatiently and said: "It's already dark. I'm late. I've got to go somewhere else immediately. I can't stay here any longer."

"Well, what about us?" the children asked the stranger anxiously.

"You three? Well, you'd better find your own way of getting yourselves home. I'm busy now."

"But, but . . . " the children insisted.

14

The stranger paid no attention to them. Once again he blew into the air, and disappeared into the night sky.

"I'm scared. I don't like it here any more," the youngest boy whined. "I want to go home."

Luckily, the children saw a soft light shining in a distant hut. They held each other by the hand as they walked over to it. The eldest boy knocked on the door. The children said in unison: "May we come in please?"

A huge woman, who was almost twice the girl's size, opened the door.

"Where could you possibly have come from?" she asked them.

The girl spoke out: "A stranger came to our village. He carried us to this place on the wings of the wind. We've had a wonderful time eating pears, persimmons and chestnuts."

"Yes, they were really delicious," the youngest boy said, a radiant smile breaking out on his face.

"But now," the eldest boy continued, "this stranger has flown away and left us. We simply must go home immediately. Our parents will be terribly worried about us."

"Little wind children," the huge woman told them, shaking her head from side to side, "I'm afraid that the stranger you're talking about is my son. He's the South Wind and he's forever up to tricks and mischief. What's more he's terribly moody. He keeps changing his mind at the drop of a hat. I've tried hard to get him to mend his ways but there's nothing I can do about him. By the way, I haven't introduced myself yet . . . I'm the Wind Goddess."

"Please, Wind Goddess," the girl asked gently, "can you help us?"

"Of course I can, little wind children," the Wind Goddess told her reassuringly. "Of course I can. Now, don't worry about a thing. I'll send you all home on the wings of my good son, the North Wind."

"Oh, thank you, thank you so much," the youngest boy said eagerly. He was longing to get back to his mother and to his own bed.

"But," said the Wind Goddess, "I most certainly won't let you travel on empty stomachs. Come into my house. I've got just the thing for you . . . I'm sure you'll enjoy my top quality rice and

hot bean paste soup."

The children happily accepted the Wind Goddess's offer. They ate and ate to their heart's content. The food was simply delicious.

When they had finished their meal, the Wind Goddess went off to the room next door to wake up her son, the North Wind. He willingly agreed to take the children back to their village.

When everyone was ready to take flight, the North Wind extended his long tail so that the three children could climb on to it. They held on tight. The North Wind blew into the air and started flying into the night sky.

They flew over the full golden moon. They flew in and out between countless constellations of bright, shining, silver stars. They had a marvellous flight. After some time they landed just where they had first taken off . . . in front of the temple of their village.

The children's parents and all the villagers, who also loved the children dearly, had been looking for them high and low. People had searched in every nook and cranny of the small village and even for miles and miles around.

You can just imagine everybody's joy and surprise when the North Wind brought the children back. You can also imagine how happy the three children were to be reunited with their parents.

The children had, as you know, eaten food they had never had before to their heart's content. When they told everyone of their adventure they spoke of it as of a wonderful treat.

But when they thought a little more deeply about what had happened to them they understood that they had learnt a great lesson from nature. They had learnt that winds can change their minds and be unpredictable. What is more important still, they had learnt that although you can be taken away, you can also be brought back.

As the children put their heads on their pillows that night, in their own homes, they looked at the night sky, the moon and the stars through their windows.

They closed their eyes happily. As they went to sleep they knew that they were the only ones in their village who had touched a very special world.

The Story of the Man Who Loved Stories

There are two men in this story. One of the men is Kitchamu-san who is clever, quick thinking and humorous. The other is a fat man who loves stories more than anything in the world.

In the story within the story there is a Japanese feudal lord – the Japanese call him a Daimyō. Then there is, above all, a very badly behaved bird.

One bright sunny day in spring, the fat man sat under a shady tree, not far from his house, on the outskirts of a mountain village in Japan. He was feeling lonely and bored and was playing idly with some stones that lay at his feet.

Luckily, after a while, the fat man saw Kitchamu-san in the far off distance. Kitchamu-san was on his way to the forest to collect mushrooms.

The fat man who loved stories got up swiftly, waved to Kitchamu-san and shouted: "Ohayō! Ohayō gozaimasu." (That's "good morning" in Japanese.)

Kitchamu-san put his head down and thought: "Oh no! That's the fat man who loves stories. He'll probably try to get hold of me and plague the life out of me until I tell him a story."

That is just what the fat man did.

The minute Kitchamu-san got within ten feet of him, the fat man shouted out: "Kitchamu-san, Kitchamu-san, please, please tell me a story. A story about something that happened long ago."

Kitchamu-san, who was in a hurry to get his mushrooms so that his wife would have the time to cook them for lunch, decided to take the fat man's request firmly in hand.

"Look!" he told the fat man bossily. "You're sitting all by

19

yourself under that tree because no one, but no one, wants to tell you stories any more."

"But, but," the fat man said sheepishly, "I love stories. I'd do anything to hear an old story."

"We all love the old stories of our country. But the reason no one will have anything to do with you any more is because every time, but every single time, anybody tells you a story, whatever the story is, you keep saying when it ends, 'But that's impossible!' You do that every single time."

"Kitchamu-san," the fat man said earnestly, "Kitchamu-san, just tell me one little story and . . . I promise you, on my word of honour, that I will not say 'but that's impossible' when you've finished it."

"Promises are not good enough," Kitchamu-san told him airily.

As you know, Kitchamu-san was no fool. He rapidly used his wits to make a deal with the fat man that he was quite sure he would win.

"I'll make a deal with you. I'll tell you a story about something that happened long ago, on condition that, at no point during my story, beginning, middle or end, will you say 'but that's impossible.' If you do, you'll have to give me a sack of rice."

The fat man's eyes lit up. "Kitchamu-san, that's brilliant! It's a deal! You can have your sack of rice if I lose, but I can assure you I will try my very best not to say, 'But that's impossible.' Sit down. Sit down, Kitchamu-san, and tell me your story please."

Kitchamu-san crossed his legs and settled himself comfortably in front of the fat man. He narrowed his eyes and remained perfectly still before casting his spell on the fat man.

"Long, long ago, in old Japan, there lived a proud, powerful and respected Daimyō who was on his way to Edo (it's called Tōkyō today) to pay his annual respects to the Shōgun. As you *ought* to know," Kitchamu-san told the fat man condescendingly, "every single year all the daimyōs had to go to Edo with their retinue in great pomp and circumstance, loaded with magnificent presents to visit the Shōgun, the supreme ruler of all Japan. That was the Shōgun's clever way of keeping the daimyōs under control. They could not take their wives or children with them, and the trip to Edo was so long and so expensive that they always came back to their domains poorer and weaker."

"I know that. I know that. Everyone knows these things," the fat man said impatiently. "Do go on."

"Well," Kitchamu-san continued, "the Daimyō in our story happened to be, on a bright sunny day just like this one, in all his splendour, which means, magnificent clothing, flags and swords and what have you, riding in his palanquin on top of a mountain pass. He was happily looking at the beautiful scenery as he sat in his highly decorated palanquin, being carried by no less than six men.

"Suddenly, in the middle of a bright, blue, cloudless sky, just above the Daimyō's palanquin, a bird started circling overhead.

"It cried, 'Peeryohō. Peeryohō. Peeryohō,' endlessly as it waltzed around.

"After some time, the Daimyō became irritated by this constant noise so he shouted out: 'Stop the palanquin!'

"The palanquin bearers immediately stopped dead in their tracks. The Daimyō got out of his palanquin to look up at the sky and, I really don't know what could possibly have got into the stupid bird's head, but . . . he let out a huge, wet dropping, SMACK on the Daimyō's black hakama that covered his kimono from the waist down.

"The retainers were deeply shocked. They jumped to attention, horrified because their lord's clothing had been so disgustingly dirtied and said: 'My lord! My lord! We will shoot this dreadful bird with our bows and arrows. We'll aim at him, one and all.'

"To which the Daimyō calmly replied: 'That's all right. There's nothing to worry about. It's only a bird, leave it in peace. All you have to do is bring me a fresh, clean hakama.'

"Without more ado the retainers obeyed the Daimyō's orders. He happily changed his hakama.

" 'Now, on towards Edo,' the Daimyō ordered, and the procession resumed its journey."

"Oh, that's good," the fat man said with relief.

Kitchamu-san continued: "It was not long before the wretched bird was back. Once again it started circling over the Daimyō's palanquin. 'Peeryōhō. Peeryōhō. Peeryōhō,' it cried again and again and again with irritating insistence. The bird simply would not go away. The Daimyō tried his best to ignore the wretched bird, but couldn't, and so once again he said loudly: 'Stop the palanquin!' Then thought: 'This time I'll get the better of that wretched bird. I won't step out of the palanquin. I'll simply lean out and save my hakama.' The minute the Daimyō did that, the bird cried, 'Peeryōhō' as it let out an even bigger, wetter dropping bang on to the hilt of the Diamyō's beautifully carved family sword that had been made by the most famous swordsmith in all Japan.

"Now it is a very well known fact that the sword is considered to be the soul of a samurai (which is what the Daimyō was). The retainers panicked. 'My lord! My lord!' they gasped, 'We'll shoot that bird. It can't be allowed to live a second longer . . . ' "

The fat man panicked too. He couldn't bear it any longer so he blurted out: "Kitchamu-san, but . . ."

"But what?" Kitchamu-san prodded him on, gleefully thinking about his sack of rice.

The fat man too remembered the sack of rice. He put his hands in front of his mouth, then said: "But nothing. Do go on with the story."

"All right then, I'll do that," Kitchamu-san said grudgingly. "Now, where was I? Oh yes, the sword. Well, to the retainers' surprise, when the Daimyō's sword was dirtied, he was not in the least bit angry. He calmly told the people around him: 'Please don't worry about that. It isn't the end of the world. Just bring me another, clean sword.'

"The retainers rushed to obey his orders. The Daimyō changed swords, got back into his palanquin and shouted out once again: 'On towards Edo!'

"The procession happily went downhill and uphill until it got to another mountain pass. Everybody had been feeling quite calm for some time . . . when . . . for the *third* time, the wretched bird, the very same one, appeared once again over the Daimyō's palanquin.

"On and on and on it flew circling overhead. And . . . on and on and on it shrieked, 'Peeryōhō. Peeryōhō. Peeryōhō.'

"I can assure you that the Daimyō did his very best to ignore it but the constant shrieking became too much . . . even for the controlled Daimyō. So, once again, he ordered: 'Stop the palanquin!'

"This time the Daimyō did not get out. He did not lean the upper part of his body out of the palanquin . . . he merely stuck his head out to stare at the bird and . . . what do you think happened?" Kitchamu-san paused slyly.

The fat man was mesmerized by Kitchamu-san's story. His mouth was open. He simply stared blankly and did not say a word.

"Well," Kitchamu-san resumed, "for the third time the bird followed the call of nature and let out the biggest dropping of all, SMACK, onto the Daimyō's forehead."

Kitchamu-san stopped speaking. He waited for the fat man to say, "But that's impossible". But the fat man was so riveted by the story that he did not say a word.

"So," Kitchamu-san continued, "as you can imagine, the retainers were at their wits' end. They discussed loudly among themselves. Three of them had their bows and arrows ready to shoot the bird within seconds of the Daimyō's possible command.

"In the meantime, the Daimyō, who had closed his eyes when he received the dropping on his forehead, slowly opened up his right eye.

"With the calmest voice ever, afraid either to move his face or open his other eye, he said: 'Please don't worry. Don't worry. All of you. It isn't a problem. Quickly bring me another head . . . a fresh, clean one, please.'

"The retainers bowed humbly and rushed off to obey their master's orders. A clean, fresh head was brought to the Daimyō.

"The Daimyō swiftly removed his sword and with one precise stroke, cut off his dirty head and replaced it with the fresh, clean head. It had just had its hair washed. The Daimyō moved his new head from side to side, in order to adjust it comfortably to his neck. Yes, it felt good. 'That will do now,' he told his retainers with a smile and then added gently, 'Now, on towards Edo.'

"The procession once again started off towards Edo. The bird flew away and was never seen again."

The fat man who, unlike Kitchamu-san was extremely slow-witted, started to see pictures going through his mind. Pictures of the splendid procession, the Daimyō, the bird, the hakama, the sword, the head, the change of head . . . the change of head! That was too much. Far too much.

Uncontrollably, the fat man blurted out: "But, Kitchamu-san . . ."

"Yes?" asked Kitchamu-san raising his eyebrows in expectation.

"But, Kitchamu-san, the head, the head . . . But that's impossible!"

"But that's impossible?" Kitchamu-san repeated slyly. He paused and then said quietly: "My sack of rice please."

"That was a truly expensive story," the fat man had to admit, "but it was a really good one and I thoroughly enjoyed myself."

He was beaming from ear to ear. In his opinion a good story was even better than a good meal. So he said: "Kitchamu-san, a deal is a deal. Please come to my house and collect your sack of rice and . . . by the way . . . thank you very, very much."

The Legend of Moody Mount Iwate

In Tōhoku, in the north-eastern part of Japan, there is a tall, proud mountain with a flattish top. It is called Mount Iwate. Mount Iwate does not stand alone but is surrounded by other mountains that rise mysteriously around him out of the mist. To the people of Tōhoku, these mountains are not ordinary mountains. They have not just stood there for centuries and centuries. Like us, they have feelings. They love and change their minds, get upset and wait.

That is why there is a story to tell about Mount Iwate.

Long, long ago, Mount Iwate stood very much as it does today, tall, proud and very powerful. Mount Iwate was very much respected by all the other mountains. He was, to other mountains, what the lion is to other animals . . . a King.

Close to Mount Iwate stood the gentlest of mountains. Her name was Mountain of the Divine Princess. She certainly had a divine sort of beauty about her and was as gentle as Mount Iwate was strong. In the spring, when lilies of the valley and other spring flowers covered her sides like a precious kimono, she was a sight to behold, and whenever he looked at her Mount Iwate found it hard to control the beating of his heart.

Mount Iwate had stood for hundreds of years looking with enchantment at the seasonal changes that took place on The Mountain of the Divine Princess's gentle slopes. After all, mountains have time to spare. They believe that as long as the Planet Earth exists they can just stand and stand till the end of time.

* * *

One day, in the autumn, when the sun was shining in a clear, crisp blue sky, Mount Iwate heard his heart beating really loudly again. He spoke tenderly to the gentle Mountain of the Divine Princess and said: "This year your autumn coat is the most beautiful one I have ever seen. The variety and subtlety of your colours takes my breath away. Divine Princess, I do not wish to be alone any longer. Will you please marry me?"

When the Mountain of the Divine Princess heard Mount Iwate's request her heart began to beat even louder than his. The leaves on the maple trees covering her slopes turned redder than they already were as they blushed with her.

"Oh, Mount Iwate. I never thought that a mountain as respected as you are would think of me. Well, yes, of course . . . it would be an honour to be your wife."

So it happened that, on a beautiful, crisp autumn day, Mount Iwate became engaged to the Mountain of the Divine Princess.

Unfortunately, their engagement lasted for a terribly long time, even for mountains who, as has already been mentioned, feel that they have lots and lots of time to spare. The engagement lasted for years, for decades, for centuries.

But long engagements are not such good things . . . neither for mountains nor for people. As time went by, Mount Iwate found that he got bored with the Mountain of the Divine Princess's gentle and subtle beauty. He started to notice the stunning elegance of Mount Hayachine. He kept looking at Mount Hayachine and found that he gradually became obsessed with her. He even began to speak to himself out loud and said things like: "I cannot get Mount Hayachine out of my head. She is so tall and so very stately. I just love the way her head touches the clouds. I love the way the mist forms a necklace around her neck. And whenever the snow falls on top of her, I am absolutely dazzled by her beauty. Oh what shall I do?"

His engagement to the Mountain of the Divine Princess became a millstone around his neck.

One dismal, rainy day Mount Iwate plucked up his courage and decided to tell the Divine Princess the truth: "Gentle Mountain of the Divine Princess," he started to say earnestly. "We have for some time now been engaged to each other. In all that time I have never done you any harm. If ever I married you I would certainly harm you. I'm afraid I don't love you any longer. You see, I can't help it but I've fallen in love with another mountain. Please forgive me but I would like to break off our engagement. To be honest, it is Mount Hayachine that I would like to live with for the rest of my life and not you."

Of course, the Mountain of the Divine Princess was no fool. She had noticed for a long time now that Mount Iwate did not care for her any longer but she had never dreamt that he would ever break off their engagement. She had secretly hoped that he would end up by getting bored with Mount Hayachine and that he would eventually love her again and marry her. His words came as a real shock to her.

"Mount Iwate ... you ... How can you speak to me that way!" she shouted. "We have been together for so many years now – how can you ever think of getting rid of me? Here! Here! Take this!"

The Divine Princess gave a heartrending cry as she impulsively pulled out a clump of her lovely, long hair and flung it violently at him. Mount Iwate was stunned.

"What are you doing to me?" he shouted back.

He was really furious. The Mountain of the Divine Princess's hair had hit him really hard and had stuck to his side good and proper. In fact, her hair became the Forest of Iomori that you can see clinging to Mount Iwate until today. Mount Iwate wanted desperately to explode. He was known to have a violent temper if provoked. But this time he tried his best to control himself and said angrily but not explosively: "Divine Princess, you have got me stuck with a forest I did not have before. You just wait and see. Mount Hermit Messenger! Mount Hermit Messenger!" he called out impatiently, "I want to speak to you immediately."

Mount Hermit Messenger answered the call ... immediately. He was simply terrified of the proud, dominant, impatient Mount Iwate.

"Mount Hermit Messenger, there's something you've just got to do for me without delay," Mount Iwate said imperiously.

"I shall be honoured to do whatever it is in my power to do for you, Mount Iwate, and as best I can. What is it that you require so very urgently?" Mount Hermit Messenger asked respectfully.

"A very simple thing indeed," Mount Iwate answered. "Come closer, it's a secret. I don't want any other mountains to hear. You see, I'm bored to tears with the Divine Princess. She doesn't want to understand that. She doesn't want to help me out. Well, if she's that stubborn I want you to take her out of my sight. Take her far, far away. I don't want to see her ever again."

"B-b-but, b-b-but . . . " Mount Hermit Messenger stammered. What a terribly difficult task Mount Iwate had set him! "B-b-but, Mount Iwate, are you quite sure that if I do what you order me to do, you will not change your mind later?"

"You just do as I say. On the double," Mount Iwate bellowed. "What's more, if you don't obey me at once, I'll see to it that you're beheaded. Tell you what. I'll even behead you myself!"

Poor Mount Hermit Messenger shook with fear. He was a good looking mountain and was quite vain and very proud of his top. He certainly did not like the idea of having it chopped off. So he had to do as he was told. It was no easy task for him to move about. Mountains are rather bulky things but he somehow managed to get to the Divine Princess's side. As he approached her, he greeted her courteously. He asked about her health. He spoke about the weather. He gossiped about other mountains. He fidgeted about.

The Divine Princess was no fool. She suspected that he had been sent to her on a mission. After he had completed all his greetings she said: "I am honoured by your visit and pleased to speak with you. But could you please tell me, Mount Hermit Messenger, the reason why you have come to see me. You must admit your visit is unusual. You usually stay in your place."

Mount Hermit Messenger found it impossibly difficult to tell her the truth. He hated to hurt her feelings. He talked to her a little more about the weather. He began to speak about a most violent storm that was due to break out soon and concluded by saying: "All things considered, Divine Princess, don't you think it would be better if you moved to another place. I can assure you you'd be much happier there and safer. You see if you go to the place I have in mind, the winds won't be able to get at you so easily and your gentle slopes will suffer no damage. You'd even be able to . . . "

"Please don't say another word," the Divine Princess interrupted pleadingly. Her tears began to flow rapidly. "Do you

think I have not understood why you have come? I know only too well that Mount Iwate has sent you to me so that he can have Mount Hayachine all to himself. Oh I can't bear it. I love him so. I've loved him for many years. In the beginning it was so beautiful between us. Oh, what shall I do? Please, please help me."

Soon the Divine Princess's tears gushed into raging rivers down her slopes. The sadness of her story and situation made Mount Hermit Messenger cry too. Together they cried for a long, long time. Their tears formed rivers that mixed together at the bottom of their slopes.

Mount Hermit Messenger had almost run out of tears when he told her: "Fair Divine Princess. My dearest wish is to protect you forever. Please rest assured that if ever you need me I shall rush to be by your side immediately. Now, please trust me, I beg of you. Come with me."

Gently Mount Hermit Messenger led her to a place that is just beyond the Kitakami river. Yes, he moved her. But not far at all. In fact, not far enough. He simply did not have the heart to.

The next morning Mount Iwate woke up in the best of moods. He had dreamt of Mount Hayachine all night long and was convinced that he would soon be able to make her his bride. For good measure, he checked to see that the Divine Princess was well out of his sight. You can imagine his surprise when he discovered that his order to Mount Hermit Messenger had not been strictly obeyed.

"I can't believe my eyes!" Mount Iwate thundered. "She has the cheek to stand there next to the Kitakami river. I can still see her . . . almost all of her. I shall not stand that. Mount Hermit Messenger . . . Mount Hermit Messenger . . . I wish to speak to you at once."

"What is it, Mount Iwate?" Mount Hermit Messenger said, beside himself with fear.

"I warned you!" Mount Iwate yelled. "I warned you!" and with one fell swoop, true to his threat, he chopped off Mount Hermit Messenger's head.

Today, of course, you will see that Mount Hermit Messenger has the flattest of tops. What's more, there, next to him, is a small

mountain with a pointed top. That is obviously his old head which the people of Tōhoku now call Mount Kurakake.

As for Mount Iwate, he had tried hard to keep his temper down for many years, but this was the last straw. He started to boil and bubble inside himself . . . uncontrollably. He threw long, hot flames out of his mouth. Smoke and ash came out of his breath so violently that the whole area was covered with lava and ash. People were absolutely terrified of him and ran away as fast as they could.

The Divine Princess did not move.

She just looked on.

Mount Iwate found it extremely difficult to calm down. Every time he thought of his situation he kept getting uncontrollably angry . . . over and over again.

People say that he remained angry for all of thirty-three years. So very angry that flames, smoke and lava came out of him ninety-four times! Historians have recorded his bursts of anger and we know that they took place from the year 1686 to the year 1719.

Well, the story of Mount Iwate and his loves does not really end here.

Today the Divine Princess still stands near the Kitakami river. She is still waiting for Mount Iwate to marry her and he may well decide to do so one day.

Mount Hayachine is still standing tall and elegant in the south with her head touching the clouds.

Mount Iwate has been calm for many years now. But with a mountain of his character and moods you just never can tell.

The Three Brothers Who
Grew Up in a Year

Long, long ago in old Japan there lived a wealthy and highly respected man. He had three good sons. The eldest, who was his father's favourite, was called Tarō. The middle son was called Jirō. The youngest was called Saburō. The three brothers, although very different, grew up happily in their father's home and got on famously together.

One day, the father asked to see his three sons. He had something important to tell them, he said. The three sons entered into their father's presence. Each one in turn bowed respectfully.

"You are now twelve, thirteen and fourteen years old," their father told them calmly. "Soon you will be men. The time has come for you to leave home. You must learn to grow up. I want you to go away for a year, so that you can learn something that will be useful to you. Leave, learn and then come back."

The three brothers looked at each other and smiled. They were keen to accept the challenge. They wanted to become men.

Tarō, Jirō and Saburō quickly packed their belongings, took leave of their father, took one last look at their large, comfortable house and began to walk away from it. They walked and walked and walked for a long time. Sometimes shoulder to shoulder, sometimes in single file. Ideas rushed through their minds as they kept thinking about what they would do during that year. Would they succeed in pleasing their father? They walked up and down hills, up and down mountains, along the rivers in the valleys, till one day they came to a place halfway up a mountain where the road divided into three. It was the second day of April.

Two of the roads led downhill to two different villages. One of the roads led up the mountain.

The three brothers eyed each other hesitantly, then Tarō, the eldest, spoke: "Jirō, you take the road that leads down to the village on the left. Saburō, you take the road that leads down to the village on the right. I shall take the steep road that leads up to the top of the mountain. We will meet in a year's time exactly, on the second of April, at this very spot."

Jirō and Saburō echoed Tarō's words: "In a year's time exactly, on the second of April, at this very spot."

Having made that pledge, the three brothers parted.

Tarō walked swiftly up the mountain. It was already late afternoon and soon it would be night. Tarō was worried. There were no houses at all in sight, and he had, of course, never slept rough in his entire life. It was not long before the sky turned pitch black. Luckily, Tarō saw, in the distance, a red light glowing in a small thatched house.

"Oh good," he thought. "That is probably a place that will house travellers like me. I can sleep safely there tonight."

He knocked at the door and asked politely whether he could come in. He heard an old woman's voice say: "Who's that?"

"My name is Tarō," he answered.

As he spoke, Oni Baba, the mountain hag, came out. She had straight spiky hair that flew all over the place, large ears, two fangs for teeth and enormously long fingernails. She gave the impression of being very strong. Oni Baba looked at Tarō with the keenest interest. For some strange reason he was not afraid of her.

"I have left home for a year to learn something," he explained. "Would you please give me a bed for tonight, Oni Baba," he asked her politely.

Oni Baba looked deeply into Tarō's eyes. She really sized him up then said: "You're just the young man I need. Come in, come in, I've got just the thing for you."

Oni Baba shuffled over to the room next door and gave Tarō a "jimbé". It looked like a short cotton kimono in white and blue. People in old Japan used it as a work outfit.

"There you are," she told him, "wear this. From tomorrow onwards you can spend your year collecting wood for me from sunrise to sunset. You will need to wear this garment all the time."

Tarō was satisfied. To be honest, he had really had no fixed

plans in mind, nor had he any idea of what he wanted to learn during the year. He accepted Oni Baba's offer happily.

Day after day after day Tarō went into the forest to collect firewood for Oni Baba.

"If you do a job," he kept telling himself, "any job, you have to do it well. Well, as best you can, anyway."

So, day after day after day, Tarō painstakingly collected the firewood, tied it up carefully in bundles and piled the bundles neatly one on top of the other for Oni Baba. It was hard physical work but Tarō always slept soundly at night.

The hours went by, the days, the weeks, the months. Summer followed spring, autumn followed summer, winter followed autumn and soon it was spring again.

One day, Tarō woke up earlier than usual. It was the second day of April. He did not go out to collect firewood that day, but waited patiently outside the house until Oni Baba woke up so that he could speak to her.

"A year has passed since I came to work for you," Tarō told her after she had finished eating her breakfast. "I have agreed to meet my brothers today. Please let me go home now."

Oni Baba, who had been pleased as punch with the quality of Tarō's work, did not in the least bit want to see him go. She thought quickly.

"Look at your jimbé," she told him rapidly. "It's still as good as new. It's not worn anywhere. I'll let you go when your jimbé is completely worn out and not before!"

Poor Tarō. He rushed into the forest. He rolled in thorn bushes. He dashed his body violently against the harsh bark of the trees. He got his arms and hands and face and legs all covered in scratches and bruises and cuts. But no matter what he did, his jimbé remained as new as it had been on the day Oni Baba first gave it to him.

"What shall I do?" said Tarō unhappily. "I've simply got to get away from Oni Baba. I can't be late for the meeting with my brothers. What can I do?" His mind was racing furiously, and tears of despair were rolling down his cheeks, when suddenly he heard a little voice say: "Look Tarō. Look! Pick up the white stone by your right foot and hit your jimbé with it."

Tarō did as he was told. He did not even bother to find out

where the voice had come from. He took off his jimbé and hit it as hard as he could with the white stone. It worked! Tarō's jimbé was torn to shreds. Without a moment's hesitation he rushed back to Oni Baba and told her breathlessly: "There you see Oni Baba, my jimbé is completely worn out. Look!"

"So it is," Oni Baba was forced to admit. "It's a pity. You worked really well for me and I enjoyed having you around. I would have liked you to stay with me. But now there's nothing I can do. You have the right to leave. I'm afraid it can't be helped. Well, Tarō, you worked so well for me for a whole year that I owe you a present. Here, take that. You are a serious minded young man. This present will help you and also give you a little bit of fun."

Oni Baba handed Tarō a small doll about six inches in height. It was made of mud and looked quite a bit like Tarō himself.

Tarō took the mud doll, bowed and then wrapped it gently and carefully in a square piece of cloth. He thanked Oni Baba for his year with her and for the doll and began to walk downhill towards the fork in the road where he had parted company with Jirō and Saburō.

As Tarō walked past a small house, the smell of food wafted up to him.

"I'm starving," he said out loud, "but I don't have any money for food. Oh well, there's nothing I can do about it. I'll try to forget my hunger."

The minute Tarō had uttered these words, he heard the little doll say: "Take me out of the cloth, please."

Tarō did what the doll asked him to do. In a flash, the little figure ran away laughing and giggling.

Tarō felt sad. For some strange reason he felt as though he had just lost a good friend. Luckily, though, as quickly as the doll had disappeared it came back carrying a bowl of delicious hot rice and succulent fish. Tarō was over the moon. Before beginning to eat, he told the doll: "You are an excellent mind reader. I'll eat this quickly because I don't want to keep my two brothers waiting."

Tarō walked down the mountain as fast as his legs could carry him. Already at a distance he could see Jirō and Saburō waiting at the meeting place where the road forked into three. They were both magnificently dressed in the superb clothes of Samurai warriors.

Jirō carried a gleaming, beautifully carved sword and Saburō a splendid bow and arrows.

"Oh dear," thought Tarō, "I'm still wearing the old clothes I wore when I left home a year ago."

The three brothers were delighted to be together again and, after greeting each other heartily, they wasted no time in getting back home to their father. They bowed respectfully when they saw him again. They bowed even more deeply to their uncle who happened to be visiting their father. This uncle was their father's eldest brother and he was even richer and more respected than their own father.

"Well," the father said. "It is good to see you back. Now, tell me what you have learnt."

Jirō was the first to blurt out excitedly. "Well, father, I've learnt to be an excellent swordsman. Come into the garden, please and I'll show you what I can do."

Jirō proudly led his family out of the house and into their beautiful rock garden. Once there he threw a piece of rice paper into the pond and, with one deft, sure blow, cut the wet paper precisely in half.

Saburō, who had followed close by, was the next one to shout out impatiently: "Father, Father look at what I can do. Look at the top of that tree, please."

A solitary pear hung on the topmost branch of the tree in front of which his father stood. Saburō put an arrow against his bow and rapidly managed to get the arrow right through the very centre of the pear. It landed within two inches of his father's feet.

"Saburō that's good," their father said. "You too have learnt to defend yourself. Jirō and Saburō, you can both be considered men now."

Then, turning towards his favourite son, standing there in his tattered clothes, the father gently but worriedly asked: "And you, Tarō, what have you learnt?"

Tarō looked down at the ground shamefacedly. He was speechless and found it impossible to tell his father that all he had learnt was how to collect firewood for Oni Baba. The little mud doll that was wrapped in the cloth that Tarō kept against his stomach whispered impishly: "Tell your father that

you've become the most famous thief in all Japan. Tell him, Tarō."

Tarō thought: "It is not good to be a thief ... even a very clever one. Besides, it's a lie."

But the doll was still reading his mind.

"Tarō," it insisted, "do what I tell you to do. Listen to me. I can help you. Tell your father you're a thief."

So Tarō followed the doll's advice and said: "Father, I've learnt to become the most famous thief in all Japan."

"What!" shouted his father furiously. "I won't have any thieves in my house. I don't care if you are my son. Get out of here immediately. You ... "

"Just a minute. Just a minute," interrupted Tarō's old uncle, trying to calm his brother down. "If what you say is true, Tarō, then try to steal the beautiful Chinese lions made of china that are sitting in the place of honour in my house."

Tarō was only able to say "But uncle ... " He felt trapped by his lie, especially as he really hated thieves.

But the mud doll whispered to him: "Tarō, accept. Tell him you can steal the lions. Tell him!"

So Tarō let himself be influenced by the doll once again and said: "Uncle, of course I can steal your lions. I can do that easily, even while I am standing here talking to you."

Tarō knew very well that he was bluffing and that worried him, but he did not worry for long because he soon felt a certain heaviness and hardness against his stomach. It did not take Tarō long to realise that the Chinese lions were sitting snugly under the fold of his clothes. Swiftly, he pulled them out.

Tarō's uncle, father and two brothers could not believe their eyes. His uncle however was a stubborn man. He decided to test Tarō further.

"That was too easy, Tarō," he said patronizingly. "But I've got a real test for you now. I challenge you this very night, to steal the box that contains the thousand gold coins that I keep at home. There was no one guarding the Chinese lions, but I can assure you that my money box will be well guarded tonight."

"Go on, go on, say yes, say yes," the doll whispered to Tarō excitedly.

After what had just happened, Tarō naturally followed the

doll's advice. That night, Tarō's uncle got himself ready with military precision. He was determined to beat Tarō at his game. He took out his best sword and placed it next to his bed. He ordered his servants to stay on guard, so that his house could instantly be lit with torches the minute he gave the order.

"No one, but no one, is to sleep a wink tonight," he ordered everybody (including himself).

Tarō brought a horse from his father's house to his uncle's house, so that he could load the heavy money box on it. He walked the horse as silently as he could, but his uncle heard the horse's hoofs. Tarō approached the main doors of his uncle's house but found them shut tight. So were all the other doors.

"How on earth shall I get in?" he thought worriedly.

"It's quite all right," the mindreading doll told him chuckling and laughing. "It will be all right. Just watch me."

In a flash, the doll had slipped through a chink in the door. In and out he slipped like a firefly. First he placed a drum at the foot of the uncle's bed. Then he put bamboo flutes and gongs into the hands of the servants instead of their lighting equipment. The uncle and his servants were spellbound and could not resist the doll's games.

Rapidly and deftly the doll removed the locks from the doors, then dashed back to Tarō, saying cheerfully: "Hurry up, Tarō, hurry up. Take the money box away. Come on, Tarō. Hurry up. Take the box and walk out through the front door . . . "

Tarō, who was most certainly not a thief but a thoroughly honest person, entered into the spirit of the doll's game with delight. He had always had the reputation of being such a good boy it was really fun to be naughty for a change and to enjoy playing tricks. Oni Baba had been right. Her present of the doll was giving him some fun.

Tarō walked boldly into his uncle's room with a sure step. He could not believe his eyes. There was the uncle he had once so respected and feared beating madly on the drum with the intensity of a professional drummer. The uncle took one look at Tarō, tried to stop his drumming, but could not. So in the middle of his drumming he shouted out rhythmically: "Thief! Thief! Thief! Lights! Lights! Lights!"

His servants had already lit the house when the uncle started drumming. They did not even hear his orders as they busily and joyfully banged their gongs and played their flutes.

Tarō's uncle's house, which had once been so serious and austere, looked as though it had become the scene of a festival. People were dancing all over the place. Tarō thought: "I had no idea that my uncle's house could be such tremendous fun. I'd love to stay here and join in. But that's not what I came here for," he reminded himself.

Without more ado he whisked off the money box, put it on top of his horse and took himself back home as fast as he possibly could.

After some time the uncle, who had got his mad drumming out of his system, decided to go and see Tarō. As he walked through his house he saw his servants lying all over the floor exhausted by their music playing.

The uncle found Tarō at home, sitting on his knees and staring blankly at the gold coins in the box. He simply had no idea what he could possibly do with the money that was not his, and was eager to give it back to his uncle to whom it belonged.

The uncle approached Tarō with a twinkle in his eye and said: "I never thought you'd be able to steal that money box from me but you have. I still can't think how you did it. I also don't know exactly what you learnt during your year away, but I do know that you certainly learnt to get yourself out of a bad situation. Keep the money. It's all yours. I don't want it. What's more I've talked to your father and we both agree that although Jirō and Saburō did splendidly during their year away, you, as the eldest, should now be considered the heir to your father's house."

Tarō accepted the money and his position with good grace. He took the little mud doll that now lay nestled against his stomach and placed him on a shelf in the place of honour.

Tarō knew very well that he would never have obtained the magic doll that had helped him so much had he not worked so hard and conscientiously during his year with Oni Baba.

People who knew Tarō say that he lived in great style and remained on the best of terms with his uncle, his father, Jirō, Saburō and . . . the little mud doll for the rest of his life.

Tokoyo

Let us go back to the Middle Ages in Japan. From about the year 1000 there is fierce fighting among the chieftains.

Japan has four main islands and hundreds of smaller ones. On these islands the chieftains have their own domains and their own retainers. They war with each other constantly. They divide up Japan in the name of power and riches. They cause death, destruction and chaos.

In the year 1320 Hōjō Takatoki banishes Oribe Shima, the father of Tokoyo, the heroine of our story, to Kamishima, which is one of a group of islands called the Oki islands.

Hōjō Takatoki is a powerful man. No one, but no one is allowed to offend him in any way. Because Oribe Shima has done so, he is punished severely by being condemned to lifelong banishment on the windy, desolate island of Kamishima.

Oribe Shima is a well-respected Samurai. He has a large home in Ise, a great deal of land and many people who work for him. Now that he is alone and imprisoned in a house on the windy island of Kamishima, he finds that he misses his old life badly. But more than anything or anyone, he misses his beautiful daughter, Tokoyo, who is eighteen years old.

To Tokoyo, her father is the most important person in the world. She feels absolutely destroyed by his absence.

"Here I am," she finds herself saying despondently, "I sit around all day in this castle. I don't feel like doing a thing. I feel sad and lonely because I can't be with my father."

As she says these things Tokoyo believes she hears the calm, strong voice of her father trying to cheer her up: "Tokoyo, I am alive and I am well. You must be brave. You must try to be strong."

As Tokoyo hears these words a change begins to take place in her.

"Yes," she tells herself as she forces a smile to her lips, "I shall try to be strong. I *am* strong. I may be slim, but I am not weak. My father taught me how to fence and how to practise self-defence. He let me go as often as I wanted with the ama sama, the pearl divers who dive to the bottom of the sea to collect pearl-oyster shells. This is dangerous but I am an experienced swimmer and I am not afraid of the sea. I must also teach myself not to be afraid of anything that could happen to me on land. What I must do now is leave my home here in Ise immediately and set off to save my father. I must leave as soon as possible."

Tokoyo immediately sells a few objects in order to have money for her journey. She packs some food and clothes and a small dagger and sets off with determination to cross her island from one coast to the other. The journey is long and hard. There are many mountains to cross. Some of the mountains are high. The valleys are deep. At times the rain falls so hard on Tokoyo's shoulders that it really hurts her. At other times she feels as if she will die of hunger before she reaches the next village. Her feet often hurt her so much that she feels she will not be able to take another step. Still she keeps saying over and over again: "Father, it will not be long. I shall get to you yet. I will and MUST save you."

With the sad face of her father in her mind's eye, Tokoyo goes on and on and on, for weeks and weeks, crossing one mountain after the other, until, at long last, one summer evening, she finally reaches the sea at Akasaki.

"There they are!" she cries out loud. "There they are, the Oki Islands. Kamishima is one of them. My father is there!"

Tokoyo feels so tired that she falls asleep, right then and there, on the beach facing the Oki Islands.

She wakes up at dawn to the sound of the voices of fishermen who are about to set out to sea in their boats. She rushes over to them and blurts out: "I am the daughter of Oribe Shima. Hōjō Takatoki has banished my father to Kamishima. Could you please tell me which one of the Oki Islands Kamishima is?"

One of the fishermen scowls and mutters under his breath: "It's that one!"

"Well then," says Tokoyo eagerly, "Could you please take me to Kamishima. It's taken me weeks to get here. I can't wait to see my father again. Could you please take me there?"

The toughest and strongest of the fishermen answers Tokoyo's request by putting his face right up against hers. He laughs loudly and says in a deep husky voice: "Do you think we are a bunch of fools here? NO ONE is allowed on *any* of the Oki Islands. It's the law. We've got families, you know, young lady. You won't find a man around here who relishes the idea of getting killed . . . not even for a pretty little thing like you. Find your own way of getting there. Don't turn to us!"

The other fishermen agree with him. They roar with laughter and set off to sea without giving Tokoyo another thought.

But Tokoyo has, by now, come too far and she has suffered too much to turn back. Her determination has grown with her suffering. So she makes another plan. She buys some food from the women in the village. She waits patiently for the men to come back in their boats. She waits for them to get back to their houses. She waits for all the lights in their houses to go out one by one. She gazes at the full moon. Good. The sky is clear. The sea is calm except for a gentle breeze that is just right for her purpose. She checks the boats in front of her and chooses the lightest one. In a flash, she jumps into it and starts rowing as fast as she can to . . . Kamishima.

The island is a good distance away. There are times when Tokoyo's arms really hurt but she does not give up and gives herself strength by repeating: "I must save my father. I must. I must."

It takes her until the following evening to reach the island. Once she gets there she lifts her boat onto the shore of a rocky bay. She finds a spot that is not too windy and falls into the deepest, deepest sleep until the following morning.

As the dawn light touches her face, Tokoyo wakes up full of hope. She eats some of her provisions and goes off in search of her father.

She introduces herself to the first fisherman she meets in the same kind of way she had to the others on the mainland: "I am the daughter of the Samurai, Oribe Shima. He has been banished and is somewhere on this island. Could you please tell me where he is being kept?"

This time Tokoyo receives a gentle answer but unfortunately the words of the old fisherman are words without hope.

"Look, my child, to begin with I don't know who your father is. Then let me tell you one thing. If he has been banished to Kamishima it means that Hōjō Takatoki is determined that no one gets in touch with him. My child, if Lord Tameyoshi, the lord of this island, hears that you are here he could put your father to death for this, and you yourself would be in great trouble. Mark my words, Tokoyo, you had better leave Kamishima as soon as possible."

"I cannot," Tokoyo says hoarsely under her breath as the tears roll from her eyes.

The old fisherman understands only too well what is in Tokoyo's heart but he cannot help so he walks sadly away shrugging his shoulders.

Tokoyo goes from place to place on this desolate, windy island. People are kind. They are poor but still manage to give her tit bits to eat. However, every time she mentions the name of her father and tells them why she has come, she meets with stony silence. People simply walk away. On Kamishima, the humble folk have learnt to fear trouble.

It happens to be the thirteenth day of June. The summer winds can be quite strong at this time of year. Tokoyo wanders around until she comes to a place that seems to be sheltered . . . She finds a small cape of rocks on which a shrine to Buddha has been erected. It is evening, and Tokoyo feels safe in such a holy place. She bows low to the statue of Buddha and asks him to help her to find her father, whom she loves so much. She tries very hard to keep hope in her heart as she falls asleep.

After about an hour she is woken up by strange sounds. She hears the waves hitting the rocks as usual but she also hears the sound of rhythmic clapping and the voice of a girl crying.

Tokoyo opens her eyes. Is she seeing ghosts? There, at the edge of the cliffs, stands a priest with a long, white beard. He is praying. Standing next to him is a beautiful girl of fifteen dressed all in white. She looks terrified. When the priest has finished

praying, he calmly puts his hand on the young girl's back as though he wants to push her over the cliffs. The girl resists. In a flash, Tokoyo jumps to the girl's rescue and pulls her sharply away from the edge of the cliffs, away from the priest.

"What kind of man are you?" Tokoyo shouts at him. "Why are you trying to kill her? What has she done? What?"

The priest takes Tokoyo's hand and the girl's hand, moves them away from the cliffs and motions them to sit down. He is not angry because Tokoyo has shouted at him but addresses her calmly.

"It is obvious that you are not from this island. You do not know the story of the people on Kamishima. Dear child, I do not *want* to kill this girl. I *have* to."

The girl cries softly as Tokoyo asks incredulously: "Have to?"

"Yes, *have* to. You see, at the bottom of the sea there is a monster which we on the island call Yofuné Nushi. He creates the most terrible storms at times and has already killed many of our fishermen. In order to keep Yofuné Nushi calm and happy, we have for many years now on this day, the thirteenth day of June, the Day of the Dog, some time between eight and nine o'clock in the evening, sacrificed to him the most beautiful girl on the island. She must always be just under fifteen years old. It is sad that a girl has to die every year, but I am sure you understand that if one girl can save the lives of many fishermen, she must die. My child, I can assure you that I do not want to kill young girls, but unfortunately, that is just what I've had to do for the past seven years."

As Tokoyo listens attentively to the priest's story, an idea comes to her mind.

"Holy priest," she says quietly, "I thank you for your explanation. Now it is my turn to tell you my story. I am Tokoyo, the daughter of Oribe Shima, a samurai of high rank. I have walked all the way from Ise to Akasaki and rowed all alone from Akasaki to Kamishima to try to find my father. No one on this island wants to tell me where he is. I have really tried to find him but I am told that my presence on this island could hurt him. I'm afraid I now have to give up my search. I have a letter for him and would be most grateful to you if you could give it to him, should you be able to contact him. Life has no meaning for me now that I have

51

lost hope. Please let me take this girl's place. Whatever happens to me is unimportant. Let her live and make her father and mother happy."

Tokoyo does not wait for the priest to accept. In silence, she calmly takes off the girl's white dress and puts it on.

She bows and prays to the statue of Buddha: "Please, please make me strong enough to kill Yofuné Nushi," Tokoyo says with all her heart and soul.

She bows to the priest. She bows to the girl. She places the small dagger that she had been carrying between her teeth, walks to the edge of the cliff and dives down into the sea like a bird. The priest and the girl have watched Tokoyo in silence and with admiration.

The sea waters are crystal clear and because the moon is full Tokoyo can see well as she swims underwater.

Her swim takes her back to the days when her father was at home in their castle in Ise. There she swam happily and expertly with the pearl divers. Now she is happy to swim alongside the silvery, brilliantly coloured fish. She swims past gorgeous, lush seaweed and beautifully formed rocks. It is truly magical and unreal in that green sea world. Tokoyo soon forgets the pain and difficulties of the past months.

Suddenly, she gets jolted out of her dreamworld as she swims towards a man sitting in a cave.

Out comes her dagger: "Yofuné Nushi. I'll get you," thinks Tokoyo.

She is about to strike "the man" when she suddenly realizes that "the man" is no sea monster but a lifeless statue of Hōjō Takatoki, the man who condemned her father to Kamishima. Tokoyo hates the very idea of Hōjō Takatoki and wants to destroy the statue,but then other thoughts come to her mind.

"Perhaps, perhaps this statue was made by someone like my father who had suffered and been banished to Kamishima because of Hōjō Takatoki. That man must have been a good sculptor to have made a statue that looked exactly like Hōjō Takatoki. Perhaps I had better do good rather than evil. It would be better to get the statue out of the sea."

Tokoyo undoes one of her belts. She ties one end around the statue and puts the other end over her shoulder. She begins to swim upwards.

Within seconds huge bubbles form around her. The waters surrounding her spin violently. A horrible light beams in on her. There, there in front of Tokoyo is, without a shadow of a doubt, the monster Yofuné Nushi. He is a really horrible creature. Half dragon, half snake, he is all white and about twenty-six feet long. He has scales on his back. Short legs. Fiery eyes and a disgusting, long, red tongue. He has pointed horns and a repulsive moustache that floats about round him. Tokoyo grips her dagger hard till her knuckles go white.

"Yofuné Nushi, you murderer. I'll get you now," she thinks. "I'll get you for killing fishermen. I'll get you for letting an innocent girl get killed every year. You won't be able to do that any longer. All this must end now. Enough is enough."

Yofuné Nushi floats towards Tokoyo in a straight line. His fiery eyes are simply terrifying but Tokoyo stays put.

Yofuné Nushi is about to attack her, when suddenly, with the speed of lightning, Tokoyo lifts her dagger and drives it hard into the monster's right eye. Blood spurts out from his right eye and blurs his left. He shakes his tail furiously, blinded by all that blood. He tries to get back to the cave where he has been hiding but his movements are slow because he cannot see where he is going.

"I am the strong one now," Tokoyo thinks with confidence.

She holds her dagger as tightly as she can as she swiftly and accurately digs it as hard as possible into Yofuné Nushi's heart. The waters turn upside down. Yofuné Nushi lets out three explosive gasps which make the fish, both big and small, swim rapidly away from him. He lashes his tail furiously over and over again, about ten times. Then . . . the fire goes out of his eyes as he sinks slowly, slowly like an old, old ship to the bottom of the sea.

Tokoyo waits till the monster is completely still. She also waits till the sea bed is calm again. She waits till the fish swim once again past her.

"Well," Tokoyo thinks, "I have not been able to save my father, which is what I came here for. But I have at least been able to save the island people from that dreadful Yofuné Nushi. I'd better bring him up as well as the statue so that people can see him dead and unthreatening. Only then will they feel truly safe once again."

Tokoyo undoes her other belt. She ties one end of it around Yofuné Nushi and puts the other end over her left shoulder. She gives the sea bed a good, hard kick with her feet and swims, up, up, up, up to the surface of the water.

The priest and the girl had been standing on the cliff all that time looking at the very spot in the sea where Tokoyo had dived down.

"Look, priest. Look!" the girl shouts out suddenly. "Look! Tokoyo has come up. She has a man with her and a most enormous fish!"

"Quick," the priest says, "She may be an experienced swimmer but she has still been down there an awfully long time. Let's run down to the shore to help her."

The priest and the girl run down to the water's edge as fast as their legs can carry them and help Tokoyo out.

Tokoyo is speechless. She feels absolutely exhausted.

The priest places the statue and the dead Yofuné Nushi high up on the rocks.

By now most of the people on the island have heard the news and they rush down to Tokoyo. They carry her tired body to one of their small houses, wrap her up snugly in a blanket and give her something warm to eat and drink. Lord Tameyoshi, the ruler of the island, is informed immediately of the death of Yofuné Nushi.

"You mean to tell me, that the girl, Tokoyo, who has saved us from Yofuné Nushi, is the daughter of one of our prisoners, the samurai, Oribe Shima," Lord Tameyoshi says with utter amazement. "I must report this matter immediately to Hōjō Takatoki, ruler of the Province of Oki and of the Oki Islands."

Soon Hōjō Takatoki hears the extraordinary story. He is amazed. He is not only impressed by Tokoyo's fearlessness, courage and determination but he is deeply interested by these events for very personal reasons. For a long time Hōjō Takatoki had been feeling seriously ill because of some mysterious disease. None of the doctors could help him.

Yet, the minute the statue which had been made in his image came out of the sea, that very instant, he was completely cured. Hōjō Takatoki felt fit as a fiddle again. The minute he had regained his strength, he had jumped out of bed and rode off on his horse for miles and miles and miles. He rode all alone, just for the joy of it. As he rode by himself he realized that there was only one explanation for his miraculous recovery. The man who had made the statue of Hōjō Takatoki had, like Oribe Shima, also been exiled to Kamishima. He had made the statue and cursed it so that the curse made Hōjō Takatoki ill. When Tokoyo lifted the statue out of the sea she also lifted the curse and this is why Hōjō Takatoki became his old self again.

When Hōjō Takatoki got off his horse, he told the retainers who were standing in front of the castle: "Oribe Shima must leave Kamishima immediately. He must be accompanied by his brave and loving daughter, Tokoyo. He must be protected and respected as the Samurai of high rank that he is. You must make sure that he goes back to his castle in Ise with a sumptuous retinue."

As you can imagine, now that Tokoyo is back by her father's side again, she feels safe and is the happiest girl in the world. Tokoyo and her father eventually get back to their own people who have missed them very much indeed. The people work hard to get the castle and the land back to the same good condition they had been in before the banishment.

According to history, a small shrine called the Tomb of Yofuné Nushi, the White Sea Serpent, was built on Kamishima to remind the people of the island of this story. It also seems that the statue of Hōjō Takatoki travelled all over Japan before being finally placed in Kamakura.

Now that Yofuné Nushi was dead, the people of Kamishima were not afraid of the sea any longer. The fishermen felt that their wives and children could live happily. Tokoyo and her father soon were able to leave all their difficulties behind them. They got on with the business of taking excellent care of the good and faithful people who worked for them.

The Exchange at Tengu Rock

"Baka" means stupid in Japanese.

It was not really fair of people to call Baka-san "Baka-san", if you know what I mean.

Perhaps Baka-san did *look* a little stupid, with his flat round face, constant grin and shuffling walk, but he was, in fact, not stupid at all. If Baka-san had been that stupid, I can assure you he would never have been able to play the very many tricks he constantly enjoyed playing on the people in his village.

On the day this story begins, Baka-san was sitting a mile or two away from his village in the mountains, near a place that was commonly known as "Tengu Rock".

People did not usually sit or even go near "Tengu Rock" because they were afraid of the magic powers of Tengus. Now, for your information Tengus are mythical creatures who, for hundreds of years, have captured the imagination of the Japanese people.

A Tengu's looks may vary from Tengu to Tengu but most of the time they have incredibly long noses which they can stretch out (if they wish) from the top of a mountain to the bottom and then back up to their face again. They often have feathered wings which help them to fly high up into the air, pointed chins, high heeled shoes, hats and coats.

Tengus are known to play an inordinate number of tricks on human beings who naturally fear them because they are never quite sure what a Tengu *may* be up to.

But, to go back to Baka-san who was sitting on a stone, on a bright sunny day near "Tengu Rock", you should know that, on that particular day, Baka-san was bored to tears because he had absolutely nothing to do.

"Everyone in this village seems to be busy with one thing or another today," Baka-san thought to himself. "They're all rushing about, which means there's no one to talk to. No one to play with. Hello . . . what's that?" Baka-san said as he picked up a piece of bamboo stick that was lying at his feet. "Let me just see if I can turn this stick into a flute."

Baka-san huffed and puffed into the hole at the top of the stick but no matter how hard he blew, he could not get a single note out of his makeshift instrument. "Well then, I'll see if I can use it as a 'pretend' telescope". Just as he was about to put the bamboo stick up to his left eye, a Tengu came flying by, wearing a straw coat and hat, which is what people in old Japan wore instead of the raincoats and rain hats of today.

Suddenly, Baka-san had an incredibly strong urge to make the straw coat and hat his own. In order to acquire them, Baka-san decided to play a trick on the Tengu, so he started shrieking with delight and said: "What's that! Aha! The full moon. It really looks absolutely splendiferous today. It's amazingly bright. What's more, I can see every single mountain and every single valley on it as clearly as I can see that Tengu flying by. And what's more . . . I can see the rabbit in the moon too. What a lovely surprise! Yesterday I was able to see Osaka and Kyoto. These cities are really far away from here. I just wonder, I just wonder what I shall be able to see tomorrow. To be honest, this telescope is the best telescope I've ever had!"

"Telescope?" the Tengu asked with curiosity, flapping his wings. "Is that bamboo stick really a telescope? Can you *really* see the moon?"

"I can see it as clearly as I can see you," Baka-san said boastfully. "With this telescope I can see the moon even when it is cloudy or rainy. To be honest," Baka-san added secretively, hardly raising his voice above a whisper, "there's a bit of magic in this telescope."

"Will you let me have a look at the moon, please?" the Tengu asked Baka-san politely as he hopped around. He could not stop his nose from getting long, then short, then long again, every second, at the very thought of being able to look at the moon, at close range, in broad daylight.

"If you borrow my telescope, I'm afraid you won't see a

thing," Baka-san said slyly as his eyes turned into slits. "The magic telescope only works for the person who *owns* it."

"Well, then, I'll swap my shoes for it," the Tengu said as quickly as he could.

"Your shoes! I shouldn't think that's good enough," Baka-san said disdainfully.

"Well, then, if that's the case," the Tengu said, breathless with excitement, "you can have *anything* you want."

"*Anything?*" Baka-san said hurriedly. Baka-san's heart started beating like a festival drum at the very thought of owning the hat and coat.

"Anything! I said anything!" the Tengu repeated, hopping up and down. He simply could not wait to have a peek at the moon.

"If that's the case, I'll have your straw coat and hat," Baka-san said boldly.

"Oh no," the Tengu said sadly. "I'm afraid you can't have them. You see they're special. My hat and coat are magic. When you wear them you can instantly become invisible if that's what you want."

"Well, *my* telescope is magic, too," Baka-san said defensively.

And so, as magic could be swapped for magic, the deal was struck. The 'telescope' was exchanged for the straw hat and coat.

"By the way," Baka-san told the Tengu, "you'd better wait for one whole hour after I'm gone before using the telescope. You see, it does take one whole hour for the magic to work after the telescope has changed hands."

Baka-san swiftly put on the magic coat and hat and, much to his delight, became instantly invisible. He ran away happily, laughing uncontrollably.

As for the Tengu, well, he waited patiently for exactly one hour on Tengu Rock before putting the telescope to his left eye, his hands trembling with excitement. Nothing happened, of course. He even tried putting the telescope to his right eye but as you can well imagine he never saw the moon, nor the rabbit in the moon for that matter. Baka-san had certainly managed to fool the Tengu.

"Just you wait," the Tengu muttered. "Just you wait. My

invisible straw coat and hat will bring you bad luck . . . that's for sure."

Baka-san began to have great fun the minute he walked into his village. His first "invisible" prank consisted of his giving a big, strong pull at the ladies' obis (large belts with big bows worn at the back) whenever he passed them by. Having done this, he made straight for the cake shop. The shop vendor's eyes opened wide as . . . one, two, three, four cakes disappeared in front of her very eyes followed by the sound of an invisible mouth munching them. The three customers who were buying cakes stood back in terror as the cakes disappeared and they heard weird munching noises. Baka-san stuffed himself until he could eat no more and then played his final, impish trick on the poor shop vendor who had let him eat to his heart's content. He pulled her hair so hard that it really hurt.

This was the last straw. The poor woman shouted out hysterically at her faithful customers: "Get out of here, all of you! Get out!"

She closed her shop for the day and went to bed petrified and headachy.

Soon after the incident in the cake shop, Ōtomo-san, the most elderly and most respected man in the village (who was also the most unpopular because he was so dry and humourless), walked down the main street followed by his eldest son, Ichirō, whom he had brought up extremely strictly. Everyone in this small village knew everyone else extremely well and Baka-san was well aware of the fact that Ichirō had, since his early childhood, never been allowed to make the slightest mistake without paying for it. Mistakes are, of course, constantly made both by children and by adults, and so, poor Ichirō was forever being punished by his severe father. Baka-san was intent on playing a trick on Ōtomo-san, the father, but in order to achieve his ends he first played a trick on Ichirō, the son.

Baka-san crept invisibly behind Ichirō and tripped him with his foot so that Ichirō fell flat on his face.

"Ichirō!" Ōtomo-san snapped as the young man lay prostrate in front of the temple. "Get up at once!"

Poor Ichirō got up as fast as he could, but no sooner had he taken two steps when Baka-san tripped him for the second time.

61

"Ichirō! Not again! Get up, boy, get up!" Ōtomo-san shouted.

Ichirō got up immediately, took one little step, and was instantly tripped by Baka-san for the third time so that he fell flat on his nose for the third time.

By this time, Ōtomo-san was blind with fury. He told Ichirō as loudly as he could, so that all the villagers could hear him, "Fancy having drunk so much saké (rice wine) by this time of day that you can't even walk properly! Go home immediately. I intend to punish you severely when I get back."

Ōtomo-san was really ashamed of his son's public display. Poor Ichirō, on his part, had truly not had a drop of rice wine to drink for the past five days.

Baka-san took his opportunity. With all the eyes of the villagers turned in the father's direction he finally tripped Ōtomo-san, the great man himself.

True to form, Ōtomo-san fell flat on his face, even flatter and harder than Ichirō had.

"That does it!" the elderly man stormed as his face turned so red, it went red all the way to the tips of his ears.

Turning his face to one side so that he did not have to look at the villagers, Ōtomo-san shamefacedly followed Ichirō home, where he hid for the rest of the day.

Baka-san had had a wonderful time at the cake shop, and a splendid time with Ōtomo-san and Ichirō, but that was not enough. He looked around to see what fresh pranks he could play. It was not long before he found his new victims.

He managed to have the villagers jump out of their skins when they heard a loud voice (with no body) shout out: "Fish! Fish! Fish!"

There, crowded around a fishmonger's stall was a group of villagers who jostled busily with each other as they individually and expertly handled the fish in an attempt to buy the freshest and fattest ones.

Baka-san pushed the fishmonger roughly aside and swiftly took his place in order to remove the fish from the villagers' hands one by one. He methodically exchanged one fish for the other so that no one was left with the original fish that he or she had so painstakingly chosen. The villagers became furious with each other as they unsuccessfully tried to get their own fish back.

"You're an idiot!" a stout, tough woman told a thin, wiry man as she socked him in the eye.

"Don't you dare!" a teenager said to the strongest man in the village, hitting him hard in the stomach with a smelly wet fish.

"I'll get you for this!" said the schoolteacher to the doctor, bonking him on the head with his brush and ink holder.

And so it went on and on and on. The area around the fishmonger's stall became the setting for a complete free for all. Absolutely everyone started fighting with everyone else and fishes of all kinds, both large and small, flew all over the place. The invisible Baka-san craftily chose the most chaotic moment of the fight to pick up the fattest and most prized fish to take home to his wife. He was pleased as punch with his acquisition, largely because he had got it for free. Feeling reasonably tired from the morning's excitement, Baka-san decided it was time to go home for lunch and a little nap. As he pushed back the screen door of his small house, he called out cheerfully: "Tadaima!" Which means, "I'm back!"

Baka-san got no answer from his wife Chio-san. For a fraction of a second he wondered if his voice had disappeared just as his body had. That, of course, was certainly not the case. Chio-san was not at home to answer his call simply because her neighbours had asked her over to their house in order to give her the news about all the terrible goings on in the village, particularly those relating to the strange incidents at the cake shop and at the fishmonger's. The villagers desperately feared that some strange, ominous invisible devil had arrived in their village in order to plague the life out of them. Chio-san's absence did not bother Baka-san in the least. He happily plonked his prize fish down on the kitchen table, carefully placed his precious straw coat and hat in the cupboard and quietly went into his room to lie on his mattress and go to sleep.

Baka-san felt no hunger pangs in the land of dreams. Even though he had not had lunch, he had eaten enough cakes to keep the wolf from the door for quite a few hours and consequently slept undisturbed till evening, dreaming sweet dreams of future mischief.

When Chio-san came home after having gossiped to her heart's content with her talkative neighbours, she was most surprised to find, in her tiny kitchen, a huge fish staring her in the eye with its big black eye.

"How wonderful!" she exclaimed happily. "Baka-san has chosen a most excellent fish today." Chio-san made no connection between the fish on her table and the incident at the fishmonger's she had just heard about.

Chio-san went to the cupboard to collect her apron, and was immensely surprised to find a dirty old straw coat and hat lying on top of a fresh pile of clothes that she had so painstakingly washed the day before.

"What a disgusting smell!" she muttered to herself, "I certainly won't have *that* in my house. If Baka-san wants a new straw coat and hat surely he can do better than come home with these filthy old things!"

Without more ado, Chio-san set about lighting a roaring fire. Having done so, she picked up Baka-san's precious belongings with the tips of her fingers and threw them mercilessly into the fire. It was not long before the magic garments crackled and turned into a heap of ashes.

Towards evening, Baka-san woke up and, without even looking for Chio-san, made a beeline for the cupboard. The magic garments had disappeared. "Where's my straw coat and hat?" he thundered at the top of his voice.

Chio-san, who was quietly sitting down sewing some clothes, replied with great calm: "Do you mean those filthy things? If you really want them that badly you can look for them in the fireplace."

"How can you say a thing like that!" Baka-san shouted as he stared at the heap of ashes. "These straw clothes made me invisible. Invisible do you hear?"

"Invisible?" Chio-san asked with astonishment. "What on earth are you talking about?"

Suddenly Baka-san was not angry any more. He had what he imagined was "a brilliant idea".

"What if . . . what if some of the magic has remained in the ashes?" he whispered to himself under his breath.

Baka-san rushed to the fireplace and, to his utter delight, as his fingers touched the ashes, they started to disappear.

"Brilliant! That's brilliant!" he exclaimed. Bursting with laughter, Baka-san began to use the ashes to rub every inch and every half inch of his body until not even the tiniest speck of his body or head was left visible.

Chio-san did not see her husband cover himself with ashes. She was busy in the kitchen cutting up the fish. She did not see him go off to the village. It never crossed her mind that it could have been her husband who had caused all that uproar in the village during the morning.

With great, big strides Baka-san walked into the centre of the village. He was longing to find lots and lots of people to plague and play tricks on. As he turned the corner of a side street, he saw an inn in which people were happily drinking saké with their dinner.

The invisible Baka-san strode into the inn and without thinking twice about it, pushed one of the regular customers off his chair and took his place. People laughed at the customer and accused him of being drunk. Baka-san then greedily helped himself to rice, fish, vegetables and soup and began eating happily at a frantic pace.

The astounded innkeeper could not believe his eyes when he saw some of the food, that had been so carefully cooked, begin to disappear. Chopsticks seemed to be dancing in the air. Slurping noises could be heard as the noodle bowl rose off the table several times before it was finally emptied and laid to rest on the table near the dish of pickles. Fish was dipped into sauces by an invisible hand before being taken up to an invisible mouth. Small saké cups kept being filled and emptied by some ghostly presence. The innkeeper and the customers sat in stony silence as they looked at all those goings on.

One burly customer whispered, barely audibly, to the weedy octogenarian sitting next to him: "Don't move. The cake and fish devil has surely come back. When he's finished eating he may have a go at us."

"Perhaps, perhaps, if we don't move at all," the old man suggested, "the devil will think that we are not here. If only *we* could be invisible," he sighed wistfully.

It had been Baka-san's intention to keep eating away for much longer but . . . unfortunately . . . something did get in the way.

The saké.

All this rice wine, even drunk in small cups, was far too strong for Baka-san. It made him feel heady and warm so that the inevitable happened. He started to perspire and to lose control of his movements. He clumsily put his cup to his mouth and as he wet it his lips began to show. As he perspired, beads and rivulets of perspiration ran down his face and arms so that part of his face and arms and hands began to appear in streaks.

This extraordinary vision was far, far too much for the innkeeper who, in a sudden panic at seeing what he thought was a streaked devil, began to shout at the top of his voice: "Get out, devil! Get out of here! Get out! Get out! Get out at once!"

The innkeeper's hysteria was communicated to his customers and waitresses, who also began shouting at the top of their voices.

"Get out, devil! Get out! Get out!"

These persistent yells so frightened Baka-san and he became so wet with sweat that his face began to show more and more clearly. What finally made Baka-san both quite visible and recognisable was a confused waitress, who in the panic caused by the uproar in the inn, poured a whole jug of saké on top of Baka-san's head.

It was, in fact, the sharp-eyed school teacher who first recognised him.

"What! Baka-san," he howled. "That's no devil. It's Baka-san. You'd better show your true colours before we all get together and beat you to a pulp!"

The fishmonger, who was also having dinner at the inn, was only too pleased to have a chance to take his revenge on the trickster. He shouted out: "Baka-san! Baka-san! So it was you all along! Get out of here fast before I turn you into . . . fried fish . . . or better still . . . raw fish cut up in very, very thin slices!"

Baka-san simply could not wait to escape from the inn. He flew to the public baths where he longed to wash off all the ashes of invisibility that had been the cause of his misfortune. He used a great deal of water to scrub off the ashes as hard as he could and when he felt quite free of them, he soaked himself as long as he possibly could in order to try to calm himself down. Baka-san honestly felt that he had had too many emotions and too much excitement for just one day.

As Baka-san stepped out of the public bath, everyone, but everyone in the village, including his wife, Chio-san, the cake vendor, Ōtomo-san, Ichirō, the fishmonger and the people at the inn were waiting outside to confront him.

The priest, who was also there, had pleaded with the villagers to give Baka-san some breathing space so that he could have a chance to explain himself.

"So . . . Baka-san," the priest asked him calmly and gently, "Could you please tell us, as frankly as you can, exactly what happened."

"It was . . . it was . . . to be honest . . . because of the Tengu," Baka-san replied shamefacedly, and he began to tell the story of his day's adventures; adventures that had started at Tengu Rock. When Baka-san finished his long tale, the priest asked him with surprise:

"Do you mean to say that you actually thought that *you* could make a fool out of a Tengu? Baka-san, that is truly 'baka' of you. Tengus were created to make fools of us and not us of them!"

"I suppose you're right," Baka-san admitted sheepishly. He had truthfully paid a very heavy price for his pranks. He had been frightened out of his wits at the inn and had, above all, managed to turn the whole village against him. He had brought shame to himself and to his family.

As Baka-san walked home with his wife, wearing his ordinary summer kimono − in other words, without his invisible straw coat and hat, without his ashes and even without his telescope − he dearly wished that he could have his telescope back even if it did happen to be only a bamboo non-telescope. He looked up at the moon, hoping to see its mountains and its valleys and its legendary rabbit but he could not see any of these things.

The moon looked oddly round and flat and uninteresting that night.

Suddenly . . . Baka-san's eyes popped out of his head. There, flying in front of the moon, was a Tengu wearing a straw coat and hat and holding a proper telescope in his hand. Baka-san quickly shut his eyes tight and turned his head the other way.

He did not want to see. He just did not want to know.

With brisk steps he walked home as fast as he could.

The Irises of the Sixth Day

She was born in Izumo, in a place called Ooe where the fields are green and yellow and the mountains are dark and misty.

She was born by the side of a swift flowing river in which her parents bathed her every day in the clear waters that left her skin like silk.

She was born a wondrous beauty. Her parents called her Aoyagi which means green willow.

As she grew older, Aoyagi's beauty became almost overpowering. Her eyes slit into thin lines, her nose was delicately formed, her lips were red as carnations, her hair long, straight, abundant and jet black. Her body was slender and supple as a young shoot. Aoyagi was not only a natural beauty, she possessed a wonderful character too. She was extremely gentle, did not know what jealousy was and spent her time trying to make other people happy.

You can well understand why, to her parents, Aoyagi was as a blessing sent from heaven. Her very presence made them happy and they would gladly have kept her with them all their lives. But being good parents, they well knew that children must be allowed to grow up and lead their own lives and, in Aoyagi's case, marry and have a home of her own.

As you can imagine, every single young man in the village of Ooe was keen to marry Aoyagi whom people referred to as The Beauty of Ooe.

After a great deal of thought and investigation Aoyagi's parents decided that the farmer, Hōriō, would be the young man best suited to make Aoyagi happy.

"I'm delighted that you think Hōriō is the right candidate for our daughter," Aoyagi's mother said to her husband and added; "He is an honest, hard working man whom Aoyagi could count on in times of need."

"I quite agree with you," the father said. "Hōriō is a good, stable man. If, unfortunately, things should ever go wrong in their lives, I'm sure he would do his best to come out on top."

"Yes," the mother added, "Hōriō seems to have the ideal combination of strength and gentleness which one doesn't find easily in young men these days."

"Besides," the father went on, "it is well known that Hōriō is extremely sensitive to beauty. He has always been very close to nature. I feel quite confident that he will take good care of our Aoyagi and treat her well."

And so, it was not long before Hōriō appeared at Aoyagi's house proudly carrying his arrow tipped with white feathers. This meant that of all the good-looking and eligible young men in the village, it was he, lucky Hōriō, who had been chosen to be The Beauty of Ooe's husband.

The preparations for the wedding celebrations in the village caused a great stir. The villagers, young and old, seemed to be excited by the idea. Even one of Aoyagi's suitors who had been rejected found himself saying: "Although I have now lost my chances of marrying the village beauty, I must confess that Hōriō and Aoyagi are a well matched pair. They will surely make each other very happy."

The young man was absolutely right.

After the wedding party, at which Aoyagi had looked radiant in her beautiful kimonos and the villagers had drunk saké and eaten delicious fish to their heart's content, Hōriō and Aoyagi finally had the time to be alone. As Hōriō looked at Aoyagi's exquisite beauty, he was absolutely speechless. Her long, black hair fell down like a winding river around her delicate face, neck and shoulders. She was gentleness and femininity itself, and seemed to come from another world as she looked shyly into Hōriō's eyes.

Aoyagi too felt disturbed. She found herself thinking thoughts that she had never thought before. Such as: "Hōriō is even better looking now than when I glanced at him as he worked in the fields. There is a glow on his dark skin and shiny hair. His kind, open smile and the gentle look in his light brown eyes makes me feel weak at the knees. Oh, I so hope I shall be able to make him happy."

For a few days after their marriage Hōriō did not go to work in the fields. In fact, Hōriō and Aoyagi did not leave each other at all. Not for one second. The longer they stayed together the stronger their love for each other grew. They loved each other with a passion that far surpassed that of any of the famous lovers in Japanese history, or even in world history for that matter. They had never been happier and would not have minded just staying together between four walls for the rest of their lives.

But even Hōriō and Aoyagi had to eat. And if people want to eat, even the simplest things, they have to work.

So one day, it was Aoyagi who found herself saying: "Hōriō, my love. We must try to stay apart from each other for just a few hours every day. Don't you think it is time for you to go back to work in the fields? When you are away I shall keep busy taking care of the house. I shall make up some cloth on the loom which I shall turn into a gorgeous kimono for you."

Hōriō well knew that Aoyagi's ideas were reasonable.

"All right, then, I shall tear myself away from you my love and go to work in the fields," he said with resignation.

As the soft autumn sun illuminated the lovers' faces and they stood against a mountain background of resplendently coloured maple leaves, Hōriō waved goodbye to Aoyagi and felt that his heart would break because he had to leave her for a few hours. Once he got to the fields, Hōriō found that he could not work at all. Trying to dig into the hard soil was sheer misery. He kept thinking of his beautiful, gentle wife and simply could not get her out of his mind.

"I cannot be without her," Hōriō said to himself. "I am unable to work. I feel I am only half a person without my Aoyagi by my side."

Hōriō did not complete his work but rushed back to his wife shortly after noon to hold her in his arms. Aoyagi understood her husband's feelings. He did not have to explain anything to her.

"Hōriō," Aoyagi whispered to him tenderly. "If you do not

work . . . surely we will end up dying of starvation." The farmers in the village of Ooe were poor people who did not have it easy.

Luckily, it was the old village artist who solved the lovers' problem by coming up with a brilliant idea. He said: "I tell you what, my friend. I have known Aoyagi and her parents since she was a small child. I know her looks and I understand her soul. Your strong, strong love for each other will only survive if you have the power and the courage to live and work like a man. I shall paint a picture of Aoyagi that is so very lifelike that you will be able to take her portrait with you wherever you are, whenever you are not with her. In this way you will feel that your lovely wife is always by your side."

The skilled painter prepared himself to receive his model. He chose his best rice paper, his finest brushes and his most valuable paint. When Aoyagi entered his studio the old painter held his breath.

"How you have grown, my child," he told her with affection, "grown in years and grown even more in beauty if that is at all possible."

"I am a woman now, old man," Aoyagi told him proudly as she laughed softly.

"The Beauty of Ooe," the old man whispered. "The Beauty of Ooe who possesses the added beauty of a woman in love. Come, my child, sit down in this light. It will be my pleasure to paint you."

When Hōriō was given his wife's portrait he could not believe his eyes. He unconsciously touched her face to make sure that he was only touching a painting. The old painter had truly captured the looks and spirit of Aoyagi. He had captured her innermost soul.

The next morning, with hope in his heart, Hōriō carefully attached his wife's portrait to the top of a long bamboo pole. He felt more at peace within himself as he parted from his wife and set off for the fields. That day Hōriō worked as hard as he had done before his marriage. The quality of his work was excellent. The only difference in his working habits was that he kept looking up at the portrait of his wife. And so the days and the months went by as the young couple found their way of being together as much as possible.

One October day a strong wind rose suddenly and blew wildly through the village of Ooe. It was at the precise moment when Hōriō looked up from his work in the field at the portrait of his wife that the wind mercilessly blew it off the bamboo pole and away in the direction of Edo, the ancient capital of Japan – which today is known as Tōkyō. Aoyagi's portrait travelled for miles and miles over mountains, valleys, fields, forests, lakes, towns and villages, to land finally in the Shōgun's palace, at his very feet, just as he was viewing the full moon with his courtiers in his beautiful, peaceful garden.

"What do we have here?" the Shōgun asked his courtiers and retainers with surprise, as they happily sipped saké and enjoyed looking at the moon with their ruler. He picked up Aoyagi's portrait himself and said: "Surely this ravishing beauty is not merely the figment of an artist's imagination. She looks too real to me to be the fantasy of a man." The Shōgun concentrated deeply on Aoyagi's portrait. He did not say a word. The courtiers, too, sat in silence, not daring to look at the Shōgun who, behind his inscrutable expression, tried his hardest to hide the feelings of passion that were stirring in his heart.

Suddenly he thundered: "Surely this beauty is not a fox woman or a ghost. She must be alive somewhere in my country. Get on your feet this instant . . . all of you. Go everywhere into every town, village and house. Scour every mountain, every valley. Start your search immediately and stop at nothing. Bring her to me as soon as possible. I must make this beauty my own. She must be mine!"

The courtiers and retainers really feared the Shōgun and for good reason too. There was no doubt that his wish was their command. And so they wasted no time in scouring Japan, high and low. They carried banners and signs with them and promised rewards so that the people of Japan would help them to find the beauty the Shōgun was looking for.

In time their search naturally led them to the village of Ooe. Poor Hōriō had been informed about the dreaded arrival of the Shōgun's men. He rushed up behind them as they heartlessly made their way to his home and forced themselves into Aoyagi's presence. By the time they found her, the whole village had been alerted. Aoyagi's parents had run to their daughter's home in distress.

"Please, oh please, don't take her away," Aoyagi's father begged the Shōgun's men as he knelt and bowed low in front of them.

"She is our only daughter. She has not been married for that long," Aoyagi's mother implored. "Please take pity on us. She is only a child."

Hōriō thought his heart would burst as he had to watch the unfeeling men drag his precious wife away: "Oh no, no, no!" he shouted in desperation, "You cannot do that. You cannot do that to her."

Hōriō could not hold back his tears as he went on to say: "Aoyagi is my wife. She is mine. I have been good to her. Very good. You cannot take her away from me. Please, please, do not take her away from me. Please, do not take her away from me . . . please."

Hōriō knelt down and beat the ground with his forehead several times as he placed himself in front of the men's leaders. But the Shōgun's men were there to obey their master's orders. They listened to nothing and to nobody.

The Shōgun's word was law.

The simple villagers had no rights, no choice. Such was the law of the land at that time. The entire village followed poor Aoyagi to the edge of the village, past the little brown wooden houses she had known all her life.

"Hōriō! Hōriō!" Aoyagi shouted fitfully between her tears as the Shōgun's men held Hōriō back so that he could not follow her any further. "Don't lose heart. Don't lose heart!" she begged and added: "We will meet again. We will meet again. I just feel it. I love you, Hōriō. I love you. I shall always be yours and yours alone. No one will take my heart away from you. No one. No one."

Hōriō struggled to free himself from the men with the intensity of a wild animal. His strength had become almost superhuman. Unfortunately, the four, tough men were far stronger than he was. One of them, who had a square face and a thick neck hit him hard on the forehead. Hōriō collapsed onto the moist earth, his face covered in blood.

"Aoyagi. Aoyagi," he moaned.

The pain from his forehead was less painful to him than the pain in his heart. Hōriō felt as though his insides had been torn away from him. From the moment Aoyagi was taken away from him Hōriō did not know one moment of happiness or joy.

Naturally, Aoyagi felt the same way too. She lost all interest in life even though the Shōgun treated her exactly like a princess. The beauty of the endless brown and beige rooms at court which were filled with priceless objects meant nothing to her. Neither did the splendid, peaceful gardens that she could see from every sliding door overlooking the balcony. The servants, the baths, the expensive kimonos she was made to wear, each one more subtle than the next, the enormous delicacy and variety of the food she was given to eat . . . even the boundless love of the most respected man in Japan, the Shōgun himself, meant nothing to her. Aoyagi, without her Hōriō, felt dead inside. She had forgotten what it was to laugh. She was unable even to force her lips into a polite smile.

The Shōgun had won his private battle. He now had by his side the most beautiful woman in Japan. His eyes were satisfied but his heart poured out a love which could not be returned.

Had the Shōgun really got what he wanted?

As for Hōriō, he had dwindled down to nothing since Aoyagi's departure. He could not work. He could not eat. He could not sleep. All he wanted was to be able to see Aoyagi again. Nobody seemed to be able to help him.

One day his parents-in-law came to see him. It was his father-in-law who spoke first: "We hear that on National Boys' Day, which takes place every year, as you well know, on the fifth day of the fifth month, the only people who have the right to enter freely into the Shōgun's court are the sellers of iris flowers. Hōriō? How about that? It is the first day of the fifth month today. If you set off immediately with a large bunch of irises in your hand, you will find that you have enough time to reach Edo by the fifth day of the fifth month."

"You have a long way to go, Hōriō, but if you leave Izumo now you could well make it to Edo on time," Aoyagi's mother said persuasively and added: "The power of love is the strongest power in the world. Who know. Who knows. Your love for Aoyagi may well bring her back to us all."

A surge of energy went through Hōriō's body as hope took hold of him. He hurriedly collected a huge bunch of the most beautiful irises in Ooe, tied them up, slung them over his back and grew wings on his feet as he ran over mountains and through valleys relentlessly refusing to feel pain or exhaustion until he finally reached Edo . . . on the sixth day of the fifth month. To go on foot from Ooe to Edo, the capital, certainly took some doing and to do that in six days was quite a feat.

Hōriō was not daunted by the fact that he had missed the fifth day. He rushed off with his irises to the gate of the Shōgun's castle and shouted confidently: "Irises! Irises! Who wants irises?"

The passers by laughed at him: "Irises! Irises! Who wants irises? On the *sixth* day! You must be joking!"

Hōriō, his heart beating at the possibility of being able to see his beloved wife once again, paid no attention to their mockery, but shouted even more loudly and more confidently than before: "Irises. Beautiful irises. Who wants irises from Izumo?"

Hōriō went on and on and on tirelessly repeating the same words.

It was only towards evening, that Aoyagi, lost in her thoughts and her tears and her silence, went back to her room and, to her utter surprise heard, not only the accent of Izumo but the voice of her beloved husband.

"Can this be true? Am I really hearing Hōriō's voice or have I gone mad?" she asked herself as she dropped her kimono belt and rushed to the window. There, in front of her, stood the thin, bedraggled figure of the man she knew only too well. She felt her heart jump to her throat as she said hurriedly: "You? You? What are you doing here? If ever anyone catches you, you will be killed."

"Aoyagi. Aoyagi," Hōriō whispered. "I cannot live without you. I simply had to see you again. Please, please try to escape. Come back to Izumo with me."

The very thought of being with her husband again made Aoyagi totally fearless. She said: "Tonight, when it is pitch dark, wait for me at the northern end of the castle wall. I shall be coming from the gate."

Aoyagi had studied the habits of the Shōgun's court. She knew where everyone would be and when. She managed to slip away without any of the guards noticing her escape.

When the lovers finally met, they held each other tight for what seemed to be ages. Then, hand in hand, the loving couple, now reunited at last, fled towards Izumo.

Luckily, the Shōgun, who was busy drinking with his retainers, did not find out about Aoyagi's disappearance until the following morning when her maids entered her room to discover that their mistress was gone. The Shōgun tried to make the incident of Aoyagi's disappearance as unimportant as possible. He sent his slowest retainers, and only a few of them at that, in search of his beautiful captive. In his heart of hearts, he knew that if ever he did get Aoyagi back, she would never, ever love him no matter how much he tried.

And so the search for The Beauty of Ooe became merely a matter of formality and was given up quite easily. In order to save face the Shōgun announced: "As a matter of fact I am quite relieved that she is gone. To tell you the truth, she may have been beautiful, but she was quite a boring woman. She never laughed. She never even smiled! Surely I can do better than that."

In the meantime, as you can well imagine, Hōriō and Aoyagi tried to get back to Izumo as quickly as possible. This meant that they hardly stopped to rest or eat whatever fruit they could find on their way. Hōriō held Aoyagi's hand tight as he kept repeating: "I can do anything now you are by my side again. My feet feel light as air. Come on, Aoyagi. Come on. Try to walk faster. Don't stop. Come on. Please walk. Don't give up."

Aoyagi's sandals were beginning to wear out. Her delicate feet were swollen and blistered: "Hōriō, please let's rest a little by this spring. I cannot keep walking." Aoyagi begged him, her voice hardly rising above a whisper.

"Well, just for a short time, then," Hōriō conceded. "We must keep going, you know, my love. There is no time to rest. We cannot let the Shōgun's men catch us."

The sun was setting as Aoyagi gently laid her head on her husband's shoulder. She fell asleep, exhausted. The night was cold in the mountain forest in which the couple rested. In her haste to escape from the Shōgun's court Aoyagi had forgotten to bring a warm coat to wear over her kimono. She began shivering uncontrollably from head to toe. Hōriō held her tight and said: "I shall hold you against me all night and keep

you warm. You will be all right in the morning. You will see."

In this manner the couple journeyed on for several days. At times, Hōriō carried Aoyagi over rivers to spare her from having her feet frozen in the cold mountain waters. As the days went by, Aoyagi found that she was hardly able to speak from exhaustion. Hōriō did everything he possibly could to keep his precious wife's spirits up. Sadly, Aoyagi had grown weak because of her long period of loneliness and suffering at the Shōgun's court. The long flight from Edo was proving too much for her: "I can't go on. I can't go on," she told Hōriō with tears in her eyes.

"Keep going, my love, keep going, just a little longer," he kept telling her. "It will not be long before you are back home again. Just a few more steps. Only a few. We are in Izumo now. It will not be long before we are back in Ooe. We are almost there now. Please don't give up."

At long last they found themselves standing by the side of the river Ito which meant that they were really very near Ooe. Suddenly, with joy in his voice, Hōriō said happily: "Look! Look over there in the distance. Look . . . it's . . . "

"It's . . . the . . . village . . . of . . . of . . . Ooe," Aoyagi whispered as she faltered and her knees gave way. She gracefully dropped to the ground on her knees. "It's . . . Ooe . . . soon . . . we . . . will . . . be . . . able . . . to . . . "

Poor Aoyagi was never able to go on with what she wanted to say. Her face had turned deathly pale. Her eyes had a look of desperation and intense love as she looked into Hōriō's eyes. She seemed to be begging him to help her to stay alive. Hōriō's heart was gripped with the most terrible fear:

"Aoyagi, Aoyagi," he shouted. "Don't die. Don't die. Please, please speak to me. I beg you, speak to me. Aoyagi, say something . . . say something . . . say anything!" he cried painfully, as he cupped his hands around her beautiful pale face. Aoyagi's body had gone quite limp. With a hardly audible whisper she was only able to say: "You . . . you . . .," before her eyes closed never to open again.

Hōriō simply did not want to believe that the woman he loved so desperately was now dead. He kissed her many, many times on the lips as he hoped against hope to bring her back to life again. When he finally understood that there was nothing more he could do, he started to cry uncontrollably, like a small child, for many, many hours. His whole body shook with the force of his tears. He cried himself out. Then, as in a trance, he carried his wife's dead body to Ooe. His mind was drained of all thoughts as he took her back home.

The Beauty of Ooe was given a funeral fit for a princess.

After his dear wife's death Hōriō felt a pain and a tear in his heart that never left him. He never ate or drank again. He never slept.

Unfortunately, the old painter had died. This meant that Hōriō was not able to ask the kind man to try to paint another picture of Aoyagi, even from memory. So all Hōriō really wanted to do was die. He wanted desperately to be able to join Aoyagi in another life. As in a dream, early one morning, Hōriō walked feebly up to the temple at the top of the mountain in order to pray. From the temple grounds, he could see in the distance, the river by which Aoyagi had died. He held a freshly cut iris in his hand as he whispered: "Aoyagi, my love. I am coming to you now. We will soon be together again. We shall never leave each other. Never. No one will be able to take you away from me again."

With these words Hōriō was able to die in peace.

This is a sad story of course but love stories are often sad.

Today if ever you go to Izumo you will be able to see the tomb of Aoyagi, The Beauty of Ooe. It is said that, in Ito where the river flows, every year, the people of Izumo decorate their houses with freshly cut irises. They do so in honour of the eternal love that exists between Hōriō and Aoyagi.

Of course, this event takes place on the sixth day of the fifth month.

Bibliography

AKINARI, Ueda, *Ugetsu Monogatari. Tales of Moonlight and Rain*, (trans. Leon Dolbrod), Charles E. Tuttle, Tōkyō, Japan, 1988.

ASTON, W.C. Nihongi, *Chronicles of Japan*, from the Earliest Times to AD 697, London, 1896.

BACON, Alice Mabel, *In the Land of the Gods*, Houghton, Mifflin and Company, Boston and New York, 1905.

BANG, Garrett (trans.), *Men from the Village Deep in the Mountains and other Japanese Folk Tales*, Macmillan, New York and Collier Macmillan, London, 1973.

BAUER, Helen and CARLQUIST, Sherwin, *Japanese Festivals*, Charles E. Tuttle, Tōkyō, 1985.

BENEDICT, Ruth, *The Chrysanthemum and the Sword*, Charles E. Tuttle, Rutland, Vermont and Tōkyō, 1982.

BIRD, Isabella, *Unbeaten Tracks in Japan*, Virago, London, 1984.

BOWNAS, Geoffrey, *Rainmaking and other Folk Practices*, Allen and Unwin, London, 1963.

BRAZELL, Karen, (trans.), *The Confessions of Lady Nijō*, Hamlyn Paperbacks, Middlesex, 1983.

BUCHANAN, Daniel Crump, *Japanese Proverbs and Sayings*, University of Oklahoma Press, 1965.

BURUMA, Ian, *A Japanese Mirror*, Penguin Books, Middlesex, 1984.

CASAL, U.A., *The Tengu* in Occasional Papers, No. 5, Kansai Asiatic Society, Kyōto, Japan, December 1957.

CASAL, U.A., *The Goblin Fox and Badger and other Witch Animals of Japan*. Reprinted from Folklore Studies Vol. XVIII,

1959. Monumenta Nipponica, Sophia University, Chiyoda-ku, Tōkyō.

CHAMBERLAIN, Basil Hall, *Kojiki*, Asiatic Society of Japan, Tōkyō, 1906.

CHIBA, Reiko, *The Seven Lucky Gods of Japan*, Charles E. Tuttle, Rutland, Vermont and Tōkyō, 1966.

COYAUD, Maurice, *Fêtes au Japon, Haiku*, Pour l'Analyse du Folklore, Paris, 1978.

COYAUD, Maurice, *Contes, Devinettes et Proverbes du Japon*, Pour l'Analyse du Folklore, Paris, 1984.

COYAUD, Maurice, *Contes Japonais*, Pour l'Analyse du Folklore, Paris, 1984.

DORSON, Richard M., *Folk Legends of Japan*, Charles E. Tuttle, Rutland, Vermont and Tōkyō, 1962, new ed., 1985.

DORSON, Richard M., (ed.), *Studies in Japanese Folklore*, Indiana University Press, Bloomington, U.S.A., 1963.

DRAGER, Donn, *Ninjitsu the Art of Invisibility*, Phoenix Books, Arizona and Lotus Press, Tōkyō, 1980.

DUNN, C.L., *Everyday Life in Traditional Japan*, Batsford, London, 1969.

DURCKHEIM, Karlfried Graf von, *The Japanese Cult of Tranquility*, Rider and Company, London, 1974.

FEGEN, W.T., *Japan Background Stories*, Tōkyō News Service, Tōkyō, 1954.

FUJIOKA, Michio, *Japanese Castles*, (trans. John Brentnall), Hoikusha Publishing Company, Osaka, Japan, 1974.

GALEF, David, *"Even Monkeys Fall from Trees" and other Japanese Proverbs*, Charles E. Tuttle, Rutland, Vermont and Tōkyō, 1987.

GORDON SMITH, Richard, *Ancient Tales and Folklore of Japan*, A. and C. Black, London, 1908.

HADLAND DAVIS, F., *Myths and Legends of Japan*, Harrap, London, 1972.

HAGA, Hideo, *Japanese Folk Festivals Illustrated*, (trans. Fanny Hagin Mayer), Miura Printing Company, Tōkyō, 1970.

HARRIS, Omari, *Japanese Tales of All Ages*, Hokuseido Press, Tōkyō, 1937.

HASEGAWA, Nyozekan, *The Japanese Character*, Kodansha International, Tōkyō, New York, San Francisco, 1982.

HEARN, Lafcadio, *Glimpses of Unfamiliar Japan*, Hokuseido Press, 1987.

HEARN, Lafcadio, *Japan: An Attempt at Interpretation*, Hokuseido Press, Tōkyō, 1987.

HEARN, Lafcadio, *Japanese Smile*, Hokuseido Press, Tōkyō, 1987.

HEARN, Lafcadio, *Kokoro: Hints and Echoes of Japanese Inner Life*, Charles E. Tuttle, Rutland, Vermont and Tōkyō, 1980.

HEARN, Lafcadio, *Kotto*, Macmillan, New York and London, 1902.

HEARN, Lafcadio, *Out of the East: Reveries and Studies in New Japan*, Charles E. Tuttle, Rutland, Vermont and Tōkyō, 1972.

HEARN, Lafcadio, *Shadowings*, Kegan, Paul and Trench, London, 1905.

HEARN, Lafcadio, *Stories of Mystery from Lafcadio Hearn*, Hokuseido Press, Tōkyō, 1988.

HEARN, Lafcadio, *The Second Book Of Recitations from the Writings of Lafcadio Hearn*, *The Hearn Society*, Tōkyō, 1988.

HIBBETT, Howard, *The Floating World in Japanese Fiction*, Oxford University Press, London, 1959.

IHARA, Saikaku, *This Scheming World*, (trans. Masanori Takatsuka and David C. Stubbs), Charles E. Tuttle, Rutland, Vermont and Tōkyō, 1977.

INADA, Kōji, *Nihon Mukashi Banashi Jiten*, Dictionary of Japanese Folk Tales, Vols. 1-4, Kadokawa Shōten, Tōkyō, 1959-1963.

INADA, Kōji, Nihon no mukashibanashi, Nihon Hōsō Shuppan Kyōaki, Tōkyō, 1972.

IONS, Veronica, *The World's Mythology*, Book Club Associates, London, 1974.

IWAYA, *The Cancerian-Simian War*, (trans. Hannah Riddell), Eigaku-Shimpo-Sha, Tōkyō, 1903.

JAMES, Grace, *Green Willow and other Japanese Fairy Tales*, Macmillan, London, 1912.

JAMES, T.H. and **HASEGAWA**, T., *Japanese Fairy Tales*, Vol. 12, Yetsuya Hommura, Tōkyō, 1888.

"*Japanese Women*," Privately printed by A.C. McClurg and

Company, Chicago, for the Japanese Woman's Commission for the World's Columbian Exposition, Chicago, 1983.

JONES, J.W. (trans.), *Ages Ago: Thirty Seven Tales from the Konjaku Monogatari Collection*, Harvard University Press, Cambridge, Massachusetts, 1959.

KAWAUCHI, Sayumi, *Once Upon a Time in Japan*, Vols. 1-3, (trans. Charles F. McCarthy), Kodansha International, Tōkyō, 1985-1987.

KAWASAKI, Ichirō, *The Japanese Are Like That*, Charles E. Tuttle, Rutland, Vermont and Tōkyō, 1981.

KIEJE, Nikolas, *Japanese Grotesqueries*, Charles E. Tuttle, Rutland, Vermont and Tōkyō, 1973.

LE NESTOUR, Patrick, *17 Calligraphy Paintings by Akeji Sumeyoshi*, John Weatherill, New York and Tōkyō, 1972.

LITTLEDALE, Freya. *Ghosts and Spirits of Many Lands*, André Deutsch, London, 1973.

LITTLEDALE, Freya. *Strange Tales from Many Lands*, André Deutsch, London, 1978.

Look into Japan, A. Japan Travel Bureau, Tōkyō, 1988.

MARIANI, Fosco, *Meeting with Japan*, (trans. Eric Hosbacher), Viking Press, New York, 1960.

MAYER, Fanny Hagin, *Ancient Tales in Modern Japan*, Indiana University Press, Bloomington, 1984.

McALPINE, Helen and William, *Japanese Tales and Legends*, Oxford University Press, 1979.

MacKENZIE, Donald A., *China and Japan Myths and Legends*, Avenel Books, New York, 1985.

MILLS, D.E. (trans.), *A Collection of Tales from Uji. A Study and Translation of Uji Shūi Monogatari*, Cambridge University Press, 1970.

MITFORD, A.B. (Lord Redesdale), *Tales of Old Japan*, Charles E. Tuttle, Rutland, Vermont and Tōkyō, 1982.

MIYAMORI, Asataro, *Tales of the Samurai and "Lady Hosokawa"*, Kelly and Walsh, Yokohama, Japan, 1920.

MIZUSAWA, Kenichi, *Where Folk Tales are Treasured: Fifteen Tales from the Japanese of Mizusawa Kenichi*, (trans. Fanny Hagin Mayer), Laughing Buddha Press, Bronxville, New York, 1984.

MORRIS, Ivan, *The world of the Shining Prince: Court Life*

in Ancient Japan, Penguin Books, Middlesex, 1964.

MUSASHI, Miyamoto, *A Book of Five Rings*, Fontana Paperbacks, London, 1984.

NAITO, Hiroshi, *Legends of Japan*, Charles E. Tuttle, Rutland, Vermont and Tōkyō, 1982.

NAKANE, Chie, *Japanese Society*, Penguin Books, Middlesex, 1981.

NITOBE, Inazo, *Bushido The Soul of Japan*, Charles E. Tuttle, Rutland, Vermont and Tōkyō, 1982.

O'NEILL, P.G., *Tradition and Modern Japan*, Paul Norbury Publications, Kent, 1981.

OZAKI, Robert S., *The Japanese: A Cultural Portrait*, Charles E. Tuttle, Rutland, Vermont and Tōkyō, 1978.

OZAKI, Yei Theodora, *The Japanese Fairy Book*, Charles E. Tuttle, Rutland, Vermont and Tōkyō, 1970.

OZAKI, Yei Theodora, *Warriors of Old Japan and other Stories*, Houghton Mifflin Company, Boston and New York, 1909.

OZAKI, Madame Yukio, *Romances of Old Japan*, Brentano's, New York, no date.

PARSLEY, Mary, *Famous and Fabulous Animal Stories*, Eurobook Ltd, (W.H. Smith), England, 1977.

PIGGOTT, Juliet, *Japanese Mythology*, Hamlyn, London, 1982.

PILBEAM, Mavis, *Focus on Japan*, Hamish Hamilton, London, 1987.

PILBEAM, Mavis, *Great Civilizations: Japan 5000 B.C. – Today*, M.P. Franklin Watts, London, New York, Toronto, Sydney, 1988.

PRATT, Davis and **RULA**, Elsa, *Magic Animals of Japan*, Parnassus, Berkeley, California, 1967.

Regard Sur le Japon, Japan Travel Bureau, Tōkyō, 1985

REISCHAUER, Edwin O., *The Japanese*, Harvard University Press, Cambridge, Massachusetts, 1981.

RIORDAN, James, *The Woman in the Moon*, Hutchinson, London, 1984.

RIORDAN, Roger and **TAKAYAGI**, Tōzō, *Sunrise Stories*, Charles Scribner's Sons, New York, 1986.

RUDOFSKY, Bernard, *The Kimono Mind*, Charles E. Tuttle, Rutland, Vermont and Tōkyō, 1981.

SAKADE, Florence, *Japanese Children's Favourite Stories*, Charles E. Tuttle, Rutland, Vermont and Tōkyō, 1987.

SAKADE, Florence, *Kintaro's Adventures and other Japanese Children's Stories*, Charles E. Tuttle, Rutland, Vermont and Tōkyō, 1988.

SAKADE, Florence, *Urashima Tarō and other Japanese Children's Stories*, Charles E. Tuttle, Rutland, Vermont and Tōkyō, 1984.

SAZANAMI, Iwaya, *Japanese Fairy Tales*, Hokuseido Press, Tōkyō, 1938

SEIDENSTRICKER, Edward (trans.), *The Gossamer Years (Kageto Nikki) The Diary of a Noblewoman of Heian Japan*, Charles E. Tuttle, Rutland, Vermont and Tōkyō 1987.

SEKI, Keigo, *Folktales of Japan*, (trans. Robert J. Adams), Routledge and Kegan Paul, London, 1963.

SHIKIBU, Murasaki, *The Tale of Genji*, (trans, Edward G. Seidensticker), Penguin Books, Middlesex, 1981.

SHIRAKIGAWA, Tomiko, *Children of Japan*, Brentano's, New York, no date.

SINGER, Kurt, *Mirror, Sword and Jewel*, Kōdansha International, Tōkyō, New York and San Francisco, 1973.

STATLER, Oliver, *Japanese Pilgrimage*, Pan Books, London, 1984.

STORRY, Richard, *A History of Modern Japan*, Penguin Books, Middlesex, 1983.

TDK *Video Letter From Japan: Teacher's Guide, Tōhoku Diary*, School of African and Oriental Studies, University of London, 1983.

TOMITA, Kamasaku, *Japanese Treasure Tales*, Yamanaka and Company, London, Osaka, Japan, 1906.

TSUBOTA, Jōji, *Nihon Mukashi Banashi Shu*, Shincho Sha, Tōkyō, 1975.

TURNBULL, S.R., *The Samurai. A Military History*, Osprey, London, 1977.

VAN OVER, Raymond, *Sun Songs: Creation Myths from Around the World*, New American Library, New York, Scarborough, Ontario, 1980.

VERGIN, Ruth, *The Land of Iyo: A Guide to Ehime Prefecture and Matsuyama*, Aoba Tōshō, Matsuyama, Japan, 1985.

WAKATSUKI, Fukujiro (trans.), *Légendes Japonaises*, Anciennes Librairies, Georg and Duplat, 1923.

WARNER, Gordon and **DRAEGER**, Donald F., *Japanese Swordsmanship: Technique and Practice*, Weatherill, New York and Tōkyō, 1982.

WHEELER, Post, *Tales from the Japanese Storytellers as Collected in the Ho-Dan-Zo*, (ed. Harold G. Henderson), Charles E. Tuttle, Rutland, Vermont and Tōkyō, 1984.

Who's Who of Japan, Japan Travel Bureau, Tōkyō, 1987.

WORONOFF, Jon, *Japan the Coming Social Crisis*, Lotus Press, Tōkyō, 1982.

YANAGITA, Kunio, *Contes du Japon d'Autrefois* par Geneviève Sieffert, Publications Orientalistes de France, 1983.

YANAGITA, Kunio, *The Yanagita Kunio Guide to the Japanese Folk Tale*, (trans. Fanny Hagin Mayer), Indiana University Press, Bloomington, U.S.A. 1986.

YASUDA, Yuri, *Old Tales of Japan*, Charles E. Tuttle, Rutland, Vermont and Tōkyō, 1947.

YOSHIDA, Kenichi, *Japan is a Circle*, Paul Norbury Publications, London, 1975.

YOSHIDA, Keiko. *The Miscellany of a Japanese Priest*, (trans. William N. Porter), Charles E. Tuttle, Rutland, Vermont and Tōkyō, 1983.

YOSHIKAWA, Eiji, *The Heiké Story*, Charles E. Tuttle, Rutland, Vermont and Tōkyō, 1982.